What readers are sa

"*Jubilee*, outside of the Bible, is the best b... plays out visually as you turn each page and you cann... story unfolds in unexpected tragedy and tribulations, along with tri... You can feel the emotions of the characters as if you knew them personally. It portrays Jesus's indescribable love for us in such a way it makes sense. It is an awesome mix of real life, and the struggles we fight daily and living the word of God. The importance of forgiveness and asking Jesus in our hearts. Jubilee will change your life; it is anointed!" MARY MERRITT, founder of Anaya Dua (God Answers Prayer)

"*Jubilee* - a must read! Once I picked up the book, I couldn't put it down. As she does in all her teaching and ministry, Katy Pistole speaks and writes from the heart. Such is *Jubilee*, a true to life story of God's redemption and rest. Outstandingly written, and with superb descriptive detail, it depicts a Job-like character in Clay Westin who experiences great losses in his life. From there, the story gets glorious..." LINDA ANDREWS, counselor and teacher

"Katy Pistole's, *Jubilee*, blessed my socks off! It's a clear and simple message; life is hard, really hard sometimes, but Father God is for us, not against us, as we can easily assume when 'the walls come crashing in.' I was in tears, so encouraged by Katy's description of who I am to Him." CINDY SENOR, reader

"As a professional counselor for 27 years, I have well-established materials that I rely on to help my clients in the healing process. While reading *Jubilee*, name after name of clients and friends flooded through my mind of who I thought needed to read this book. Katy did a beautiful job of weaving together principles of natural horsemanship and exchanged life truths that can challenge and encourage everyone, Christian and non-Christian alike. I will definitely keep copies of this book on my shelf for my clients!" ROBYN HENNING, M.A., Founder and President of Exchanged Life Ministries of Greater Philadelphia

"I remember the evening Katy told me the outline of *Jubilee* in 2014. She painted a vivid, exciting story full of life, so the publishing of this book is something I've eagerly anticipated, yet it goes way beyond anything I could have imagined.

Katy teaches using a unique platform, and I'm grateful for her insights. Everything I know about horses I learned from her (through the beloved Sonrise Farm Series). She also taught me that the relationship between humans and horses is a modern day parable of our Shepherd/sheep relationship with Jesus. The similarities have enriched and enhanced my understanding of both.

I think virtually all Christians struggle with the idea that God lets painful things come into the lives of His beloved children. Katy is unafraid to address this concept in a kind and gentle way that is illuminated with truth to chew on. She uses the human/horse relationship to beautifully illustrate God's intentions toward us and our flat-out inability to comprehend what in the world He is doing unless He explains it to us.

Now, as a born and raised Texas girl, let me tell you I was watching the details carefully and she got it right. It brought back many memories of cornmeal breaded fried fish, Hotel Galvez, oil wells, West Texas, farmers, and ranchers. You'd think she was a native." PENNY MCADAMS, founder of Shepherd's Call

"Katy is a masterful storyteller who understands how to weave the divine seamlessly into a beautiful love story. I began the book with curiosity, then was so captivated that I raced through the middle of the book with wonder. By the end, I had to slow down and savor every morsel of truth through watery eyes. My emotions ran the gamut from anger to pleasant surprise to pure delight. There were transcendent moments that caused me to be aware of how impactful this extraordinary book will be." BARBARA ROLEN, blogger at www.pursueabundantlife.com

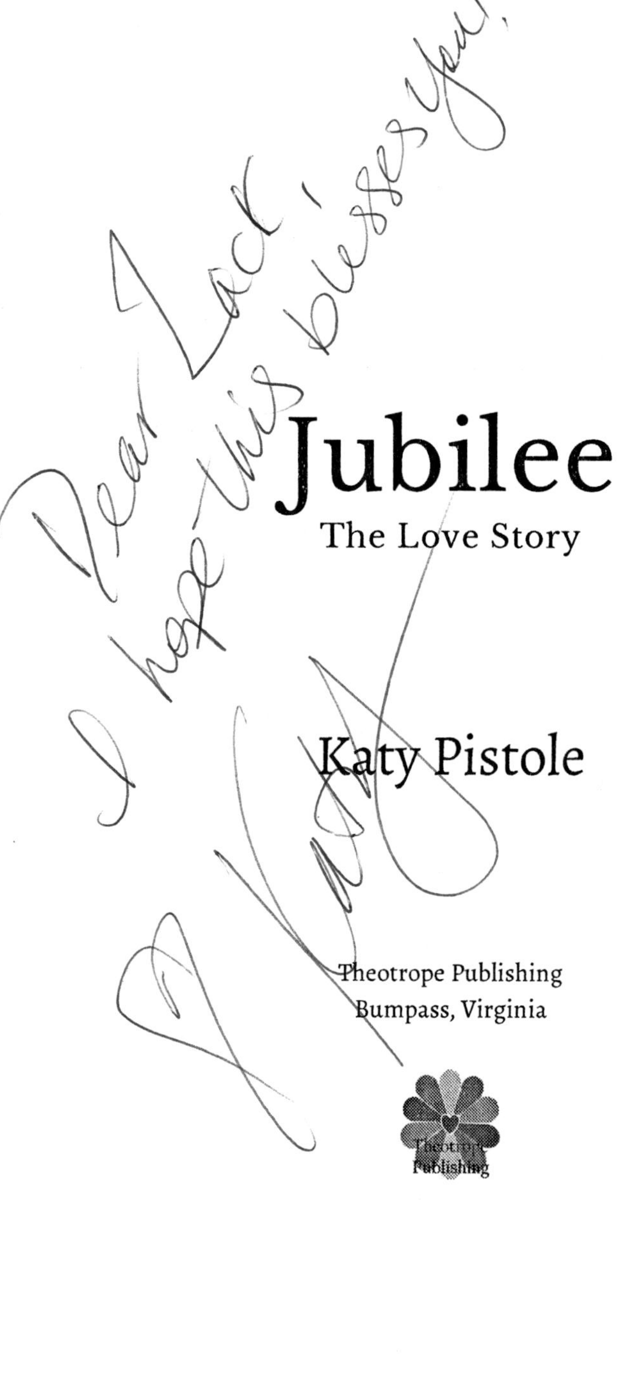

Jubilee

The Love Story

Katy Pistole

Theotrope Publishing
Bumpass, Virginia

Theotrope Publishing

Katy Pistole/Theotrope Publishing
PO Box 181
Bumpass, Virginia, 23024

Jubilee / Katy Pistole. - 1st ed.

ISBN: 1732593507
ISBN-13: 978-1732593503

Dedication

To Foufoot and Granny

Go ahead. Say it.

♥

Acknowledgements

I would like to thank many people including my parents, Sam and Judy Thomsen, who have continued to believe in me and this project through very painful circumstances.

Thank you, Ron and Kate, for sharing Life every Sunday.

And Melanie and Sarah, thank you for opening your hearts and home and giving me a safe place to just be.

Elaine, thank you for being a haven and oasis of peace.

And CC and Paul, whose gift made finishing this possible.

I would love to thank Shirley and Bob, Robin and Roger, Robyn, Ree, Zoe, and Kathie, whose regular gifts to Beautiful Brokenness sustained horses through our great adventure.

I would also love to thank and acknowledge all of my friends and family who took us in or walked with us. You know who you are.

I love you all!

Forward

Our family recently went through a period where, in three months, we lost five people who were very close to us. Long-term illnesses including pancreatic cancer and ALS, an overdose, a suicide and the sudden death of a family member seemed like just too much to process. I told my friends that it was like having the 'emotional dry heaves.'

I am currently going into my 32nd year of vocational ministry as a counselor, teacher, and student. One of my current conclusions has been the importance of the writings in the Hebrew scriptures found in the book of Job along with the New Covenant letter addressed to the Romans.

Romans logically walks through how a real relationship with God is established and maintained, while Job's story paints a personal and poetic picture of the reality and significance of pain in the life of someone who might dare to place their hope in God.

As my unanswered 'why God' questions began to fade, I was left with the pain. You see, I always believed that God was all knowing, but the fact that He wouldn't tell me 'why' only added to my hurt and confusion.

I thought I needed (deserved) an explanation.

I have begun to realize that while the answers to my 'why' questions were important, that more than anything else, I needed comfort. And I wouldn't find comfort in an explanation. In fact, I don't think there is even a Hebrew name for God that translates as 'the One who satisfies my need to understand.'

I needed Comfort, Healing, and Friendship and fortunately, He is all that and more.

When facing the big questions in my own life and as I have had opportunity to share hope with others, I wouldn't typically have run to the equine section of the bookstore looking for answers. Sometimes we need a friend who is just different enough to lead us out of the same aisles that we have been traveling for most of our lives so that we might be surprised.

I didn't read this book because of its beautiful cover or its theme. I read it because I have known Katy long enough and well enough to know that she has lived her life out loud. Without pretense or pat answers. I like that.

I'm so grateful that this story doesn't attempt to explain why bad things happen. And even better, this story doesn't offer a one-size-fits-all prescription for how to fix a problem.

Katy has captured in this surprising story an imaginative combination of truth that I have sometimes only been able to stare at when I re-read the pages of Job and Romans.

What really surprised me is that being able to cry again has helped me more than I would have ever known to ask for. Thank you, Father. Thank you, Jubilee!

Karl A. Kakadelis
Executive Director
Grace Ministries, Inc.

Preface

I see Jesus everywhere. Not in a pantheistic way, but in a child-like wonder way. I cannot imagine living this life without His constant abiding presence, and my ever-growing awareness of His Life in me and my Life in Him.

Jesus first whispered to my heart when I was 12, living in Botswana. I received my first horse for Christmas. Black Jack answered all of my little girl dreams, and I felt no need for Jesus.

But then, my horse got sick. Deathly sick. With an untreatable virus. My parents offered to gather friends to pray, and I was desperate enough to let them.

I raced to the barn the next day to find Black Jack healthy and eating. I knew in that moment that Jesus is real. Powerful. Good. Jesus has allowed horses to help me experience the heart of The Shepherd in a way that continues to overwhelm me.

I began writing Jubilee in 2004. The story played out in my mind like a movie. I wrote the words as quickly as I could, often struggling to keep up with the vision.

I used some unconventional devices within the story, the most important being the different fonts.

We have an enemy, but he does not sound like an enemy. He sounds like me. The enemy offers me thoughts that sound like my thoughts. They sound condemning and true.

I have identified the enemy's voice with a **bold font**.

Then we have God's voice. I have identified His sweet voice with a ***bold italic.***

Jesus draws me into His Story, where I find Life. True Life.

I hope you love Jubilee.

I hope it blows apart some of your paradigms about Him, about yourself and about Life.

Dancing in Him ~ with you!

Katy

Part One

Who will separate us from the love of Christ? Will tribulation, or distress, or persecution, or famine, or nakedness, or peril, or sword? Just as it is written,

> *"FOR YOUR SAKE, WE ARE BEING PUT TO DEATH ALL DAY LONG; WE WERE CONSIDERED AS SHEEP TO BE SLAUGHTERED."*

But in all these things we overwhelmingly conquer through Him who loved us. For I am convinced that neither death, nor life, nor angels, nor principalities, nor things present, nor things to come, nor powers, nor height, nor depth, nor any other created thing, will be able to separate us from the love of God, which is in Christ Jesus our Lord.

Romans 8: 35 ~ 39 (NASB)

• CHAPTER 1 •

Nede, Texas

June 4, 1993

Clay Westin's eyes stung as the blood bay colt trotted past him in the round pen. Jubilee moved with bold extravagance, tail flagged, dark eyes alert, inside ear fixed on Clay awaiting the next step.

At three years old, Jubilee no longer looked coltish. His powerful mahogany neck glistened under a mass of black mane; his body rippled with masculinity.

Clay inhaled and stepped backward inviting the young stallion inward. Jubilee responded immediately, whirling toward him.

Clay moved lightly forward and exhaled, pointing his finger to the left. Jube pivoted in the same direction, tossing his head; full of play. *Breathtaking.*

Goosebumps tickled up Clay's arms as he gave himself entirely to the dance. The horse found his stride and cantered around him, closer and closer until Clay could have reached out and touched him.

A monster horsefly buzzed the colt's hindquarters. Jubilee's focus shifted to the insect which had landed at the dock of his tail, in a strategic spot, where the colt's frantic swishing could not reach.

Flies. Clay hated flies.

A fierce protectiveness burned in his belly, and he stepped backward to draw Jubilee near. "Come here; I'll get it." But Jubilee, too focused on the fly to notice the invitation, took off toward the edge of the round pen at a gallop.

Clay waited. He knew what would happen. The colt would try on his own to escape the attack. Jube bucked, spectacularly, skidded to a stop and threw his head around in a futile attempt to bite the bug. The insect stabbed its needle-like mouthparts into Jube's blood-rich skin.

Jubilee took off again, slashing his tail and kicking out. After several moments, the colt began to look for help.

Clay caught the colt's eye. He stepped back again and opened his arms, offering himself. Jube spun in toward him, then pivoted to present his hindquarters.

Clay slapped the fly – hard. He opened his hand to ensure total extermination, then wiped the blood and fly guts on his jeans.

Jubilee released a huge sigh, turned around and pressed his forehead against Clay's chest. He did not push, he simply stood.

The threatened tears fell as Clay rubbed the stallion's face. "Oh, how I will miss you," Clay whispered.

His connection with Jube was stronger than any other horse in his 68 years. Except one – long ago. But he did not want to remember her today.

Today was a happy day.

They exhaled in unison, and Clay moved to stroke Jube's sweat shimmery neck.

"Whew. It's hot." He turned toward the arena gate, suddenly dizzy. He bent over, dropping his Stetson in the sand. He stayed that way for a moment until the pounding blood drum in his head dissipated, then he snatched his hat and straightened. Jubilee nuzzled him from behind.

"Let's get inside." Clay motioned to the colt to follow.

An overfed German shepherd waiting by the gate fell in behind Clay.

The air in the barn felt twenty degrees cooler. Clay opened the stall door for the colt and flicked on the overhead fan. Jubilee plunged his nose into the automatic waterer and splashed around before drinking. Clay smiled. The colt never did anything small or quiet.

He gazed at the horse and shook his head. Jubilee had finished up just shy of 16 hands of magnificence. Built for performance. Perfect for Josh.

Clay's swollen fingers kneaded at his chest as he paced through the massive threshold of the new barn. His heart hesitated, then bumped hard twice to catch up. The arrhythmia bothered him when he was younger. Scared him spitless if he was honest. Now the palpitations came so frequently he barely noticed them.

Dr. Purcell's voice had been gentle at last week's cardiology appointment. He asked Clay into his office after the exam. Never a good sign.

> *"We knew this was coming, Clay. You are in the final stages of heart failure. Could be a couple months, maybe more. It will depend on how well you take care of yourself." The doc looked sternly over his glasses. "You are gonna' need to slow down Clay. You'll have more edema. Might be time to take off that wedding ring. She's been gone more than 20 years. I'd hate to have to cut it."*

It was already too late. Clay couldn't budge the band even with soap. He stared into the mirror over the sink and sighed. He would rather lose the finger.

He'd made his peace. He was just waitin' on the boy.

Clay glanced back through the breezeway. *The barn turned out amazing.* Better than he'd hoped. He couldn't wait to see Josh's face.

Waiting. Clay hated waiting.

No sign of the red truck. He glanced at the dog, alert but quiet.

One more thing to do.

He returned to Jubilee's stall to apply the final detail. His hands shook so hard he had to use both to turn the final rotation of the screwdriver. The arthritic thumb burned, but he ignored it. He pocketed the tool, lurched upright, and took a careful step back to admire the silver name plaque he'd attached to the colt's stall door.

Perfect.

He took a couple more steps back and sank onto a large tack trunk, eyes fixed on the plate. Black letters popped against the luminous sterling. "Joshua's Jubilee." He spoke louder than he meant to, and his words seemed to hang in the humid air.

The dog whined and pushed his wet nose into Clay's palm. "He'll be home soon, Samson," Clay said, cradling the dog's gray muzzle. Age-clouded eyes blinked back, and Samson's head grew heavy.

Clay hadn't noticed the opaqueness before.

When had the dog grown old? "Seems like yesterday," he swallowed hard, "you were a pup."

Samson was Josh's 16th birthday gift. It seemed impossible that so much time had passed.

Samson wagged his tail apologetically and slumped to the floor, his head propped against Clay's boots.

Clay rested his own head against the polished timber of the barn, closed his eyes, and tried to relax. He inhaled the sweet fragrance of alfalfa hay mingled with horse sweat and cedar shavings.

Lord, he loved the way the new barn smelled, especially the alcove with the office and library. Like paint and varnish and books with unbent spines. Amenities Clay would never have chosen for himself. He could *see* Josh leaning back in the leather swivel chair, feet on the oak desk, perusing the *Merck Veterinary Manual.*

Bales of hay in the loft, pristine tractor, overflowing tack room. All Josh needed to do was fill the stalls with mares. And he would have the money to choose the best.

What will he say when I give him the keys? The thought made his fingers tingle. It would be better than Christmas morning, watching the boy rip into wrapping paper.

A nest full of hatchlings chattered with hunger as their parents swooped in. Clay opened his eyes then and smiled. It was good luck to have swallows in a new barn. Josh loved swallows. Took after Evie that way.

The foreman ducked through the back door of the barn, empty buckets clanking. "They're sayin' thunderstorms to-night, Mr. Westin. I moved the big tractor into the shed. You want me to close this door in case it rains?"

"No, Billy. I'll get it. You go on home to your family." Clay pushed to his feet. "I'm just waitin'." His throat closed around the words, and he shoved his quaking hands into the pockets of his jeans before the young man could see.

"I'd better close it, sir. The track is pretty sticky. Might want to mention it to the builder." Billy dropped the buckets and threw his considerable weight into the wood frame of the sliding door. The massive structure creaked in protest, then gained momentum and clicked into place. "Nothin's gettin' through there," he grinned, his pink cheeks mounding up into his blue eyes. Billy smiled with his whole face.

Jubilee's nameplate sparkled in the sunlight like a tiny beacon and caught Billy's notice. He pointed at the plaque with his well-fleshed chin. "Nice touch, Mr. Westin."

"Thanks. First of many, I hope. Put in a standing order with the jeweler in town. Josh will just have to call with the names."

Billy's grin grew wider. "I figured you'd be getting more horses now the barn is done. And Jube comin' along so well. Alls you need is some good mares – you'll be back in the horse business."

"Not me, Billy. Josh. He's got the best colt I ever bred; he'll have the pick of mares. He'll be set up right."

Billy's smile faded, and he cocked his head. "You going somewhere?"

Clay's insides turned to water. His heart hammered with his glorious secret. He needed to tell *someone*. He raised his eyebrows conspiratorially, inviting Billy to probe.

Billy rearranged his tobacco wad and stepped closer. "What are you up to, sir?"

Clay returned to Jubilee's stall and reached to scratch the colt's withers. The deep russet hair under his fingers felt slick and clean. He rested his forearms on the stall door and stared for a moment at the dust as it danced in the shafts of late-day Texas light.

"I'm givin' Josh the ranch." He turned his head to watch his words make landfall.

Billy's mouth gaped perfectly. "Everything?"

Clay nodded just once. Warmth spread through him, smooth as honey.

"That's some graduation gift." Billy removed his sweaty ball cap in reverence.

Clay straightened and allowed one side of his mouth to curve upwards. "I want him to have what I didn't. And I want to *see* him enjoy it." Bitterness pinched Clay's heart, and his lips went stiff. He pushed the memory of his father aside to focus on his boy.

Not a boy anymore. He's a man. 22 years old. College graduate.

"When are you gonna' do it?"

"Tomorrow afternoon, at the graduation party." Clay mopped his forehead with a grungy bandana.

"Guess that means I'll have a new boss."

"Yup, but don't say anything 'til I tell you." Clay turned and patted Billy on the shoulder as they strolled to the parking area. "I'll be around. It'll be the two of us. The J.C. Ranch. I've ordered a new sign. One of them big metal ones you put on phone poles at the end of the driveway. Everyone'll see it as they go by."

"The J.C. Ranch," Billy repeated. He smoothed his damp hair and replaced the cap. "That sounds right," he nodded. Billy climbed into his Chevy and rolled the window down. "Have a good evening, sir. I'll see you and Josh in the morning."

"Thank you, Billy. And remember," Clay held his finger to his lips.

"Secret's safe with me," Billy grinned and drove.

Clay returned to Jubilee's stall. The colt snatched a mouthful of hay from the pile and came to the door. Clay ran his hands down the colt's face, over the soft brown eyes, down to the velvety muzzle. The colt leaned into his hand, and Clay had to pull the bandana out again.

Something about Jubilee made tears spring up every time. Something about the whole Jubilee bloodline. Maybe it was their eyes. Large, wise, doe-like.

What if the boy has made plans in Houston? The thought burned through his joy.

Full-blown panic liquefied his knees, and he grappled with the door like a drowning man. His lungs felt brittle enough to shatter. He coughed hard and thumped his chest.

Lordy, he was gonna' give himself another heart attack.

Jubilee whirled around to stare out the back window of his stall and stood motionless, a long strand of hay suspended from his mouth.

When Samson took off, barking like crazy, Clay knew. *He's home.*

He tried to keep it to a walk but couldn't. He broke into a jog, wincing every time he landed on his left leg.

Tomorrow, at Josh's graduation party, Clay would give his son the keys to the house, the barns, the ranch, the oil. *My son will never want for anything.*

Clay burst through the door of the barn just as Josh hopped out of the truck. Their eyes met, and Clay's knees went weak again. He grasped the door and steadied himself. Those eyes, grey-green, and shaped just like hers. *Oh, Evie, you'd be so proud. He's a man. A good man.*

Clay tottered down the walkway, grabbed his boy and squeezed tight. His ear just reached Josh's chest. How he and little Evie Mayfield had produced such height never ceased to delight him.

Clay listened to his boy's strong, slow heartbeat for a moment, then drew back so he could take in Josh's face. "How was the drive?"

Josh's shoulders collapsed, "Long, Dad. I'm glad to be home."

Samson bayed in ecstasy, dancing and slobbering all over their shoes. Josh rubbed the dog's ears while he surveyed the barn. "Where's Jube?"

"Last stall on the left." Put him there so you'd have to see the whole barn.

Josh wandered up the stone walkway to the entrance. "The place looks great Dad. You finally finished." Josh caressed the wood as his gaze followed the massive cedar beam into the high gabled roofline and the hayloft. "Amazing woodwork, and the light. I've never seen so many windows."

Jubilee whickered from the far end of the barn.

"Hold on; I'm coming."

Clay hung back. *Will he notice?*

"Whoa!" Josh dropped a knee to examine the plaque. "Dad, it's beautiful."

"That's Jubilee's graduation gift from me," Clay folded his arms over his thumping heart as he sat on the oak trunk. "You'll have to wait a bit for yours."

Josh slipped into Jubilee's stall and threw his arms around the colt's neck. "No need. Good grief, Dad. You paid for school. Most of my friends have student loans up to their eyeballs."

Clay shrugged, but could not suppress a smile.

Josh ran his hands over Jubilee's well-muscled back. "He looks great." He grinned at Clay. "Really filled out. I can't wait to get him under saddle."

"Tomorrow. Let's eat. I've got somethin' to ask you."

Josh poked his head under Jubilee's neck. "I'm all yours."

Clay grabbed the duffel bag from the front seat and headed to the house, noting the dark wall of clouds and cool edge to the wind.

Storm's coming. Hope I get the steaks grilled before it arrives.

•

Josh pushed his chair from the table and unbuttoned his jeans. He had eaten quickly and too much. He lounged back, stretching his long legs.

He wasn't looking forward to telling his father about the internship in Dallas. He knew Clay wouldn't be angry, just quietly injured.

His father's plans for him were no secret, and he was excited about the potential he saw in Jubilee, as a competitor, and as a legacy stud.

Josh wanted more.

He'd witnessed the life-changing difference horses could make with prison inmates. His heart yearned to share real Life with the young men he'd met through a prison ministry at school.

He leaped at the opportunity for a summer-long internship. He could see himself immersed in a program combining all aspects of horsemanship.

The future ranch would be self-sustaining. The staff could teach the inmates to really *be* with horses. To learn how to build relationship with them, and with each other. To care for the horses, campaign, breed and find that perfect person for each horse.

Josh wrestled with the timing. He was expected to report to the ranch in a week, and he wanted his dad to be excited with him. If his father had not planned the huge party, Josh would have gone straight on to Dallas.

Tonight probably wasn't the night. His dad seemed preoccupied with something. *Maybe the crowd coming for the party tomorrow*. His father liked privacy, solitude.

Josh watched Clay fiddle with his food. I wish I could help you love people the way you love your horses.

•

Clay rose from the table, unable to sit a moment longer. He'd fussed with his steak, cut it into pieces and pushed it around. The salad and potato remained untouched.

"How was my cookin?"

"Great, Dad. Way better than school food."

Samson waited between them, his tail fanning the floor, eyes bright with expectation.

"Hope you saved room," Clay stacked Josh's plate atop his own and carried the pile to the sink.

He tossed his still meaty T-bone to Samson who clamped on it mid-air and carried it to a retired sofa cushion in the far corner of the kitchen.

"I picked up one of Dot's cakes. Chocolate with chocolate."

"Can we have it later?" Josh rested his hand on his belly. "I think I ate enough for both of us.

"Yep. Later it is." Clay wiped imaginary crumbs from the counter, into the sink.

"You feeling all right? You didn't eat much."

"I need to ask you somethin'." Clay pushed the curtain from the window over the sink to peer at the barn. As he watched, darkness activated the security light in front of the barn and gave him a sense of peace.

"Sure, Dad. What?"

Clay turned around and pressed his back against the sharp edge of the granite counter. It gave him something to focus on, made his spine strong. *Josh, how I love you; need you home.* Clay swallowed hard. "I know Eli has been talking to you about working with the youth group at church. If you could do anything - money didn't matter - what would you do?"

Clay took a sip of water and resisted the urge to close his eyes as he waited.

Josh sat up, elbow on the table, two fingers holding up his chin. It was his thinking pose. Clay had seen it often. The boy pursed his lips several times as though sorting his thoughts. Or trying to figure the best way to say something.

Don't say you're leaving. I need you here. Just for a little while. Just need you for a little while.

The boy breathed out, and Clay could see he'd decided. "I'm glad you asked, Dad. I've been volunteering at a prison near school."

Clay's eyes widened, but he forced an encouraging smile.

Josh continued, passion igniting in his face. "Some of the men - they're younger than I am - are about to be released on a work program."

Clay's heart swamped as Josh began using his hands, visualizing. The boy could see it.

"They think life is all about money, survival, getting ahead." Josh's enthusiasm flamed and he hopped his chair toward Clay. "I want to start a ranch, Dad. A place where these guys could live and apprentice. I want to bring in top-notch farriers, trainers, and veterinarians.

"I want them to have a chance to learn about a real relationship with Jesus and work with horses, the way you taught me. I want to offer them something different. Something *true*." Josh clasped his hands around the last words and drew them into his chest.

This could work. Clay's mouth relaxed. He hadn't realized he'd stopped breathing. He returned to the table, pulled his chair out and faced Josh. "Where do you want this ranch?"

"Don't know yet. Been offered an internship over the summer at a place near Dallas."

No.

"It's a great opportunity to learn the ropes. I need to report next week. I'll be there 'til September."

Too long. Clay's panic slithered up into his throat. "What about here? Could you do something here?" The words barely escaped.

Josh blinked hard. "You mean *after* the summer?"

Clay shook his head – couldn't help it. But forced his tongue to say, "Yes."

God help me.

Josh stared into space for a moment. "I don't know." He cocked his head. "I hadn't thought about here. It would mean lots of guys, activity. I didn't think you'd enjoy that."

"I prob'ly wouldn't," Clay admitted. "But I'd get over it." He softened his shoulders. "Think about it. I could help you, with the horse side of things, for a little while anyway." *I don't want to die in this house alone.*

Josh leaned forward, his eyes soft but squinty with questions. "Are you okay?" He squeezed Clay's forearm gently. "I know you've missed me, but Dallas isn't far. Two hours. And we're only talking about a couple months."

Clay patted Josh's hand and looked away. He wanted to tell Josh how proud he was, how he loved him. But he couldn't.

He couldn't.

Just thinking about it made the pounding behind his eyes build. He chewed on his lip, tried to get hold of himself.

What if I give him the keys now?

No. Clay didn't want to pressure him.

He would stick with his plan. Josh would do what was right. He always did. Took after Evie that way too.

Tomorrow. It will all be clear tomorrow.

•

Clay pushed back in his recliner and flipped through the channels. "C'mon. Gimme the weather."

"It feels strange," Josh started his words at the end of a huge yawn. He was stretched out on the leather sofa; Samson snoring under his bent knees.

"What's strange?" Clay pulled away from the evening news.

"No Hebrew to memorize. No alarm clock."

"Good." Clay said and turned his attention back to the television. "Party under the tent – or outside?"

A thunderclap rattled the windows. "I'm thinking tent," Josh said, swinging his long legs over Samson.

The dog whined and scrambled off the sofa.

Clay felt it first, a creepy tingling sensation, then a deafening bright white explosion followed instantly by an earthquake-like concussion.

He ducked instinctively in the same instant the lights and television died.

"That was too close," Clay whispered in the dark.

Samson whimpered and began to pant.

"It's OK, old man," Josh patted the dog's side.

The lamp flickered on, and they stared at each other, listening. The air-conditioner resumed its steady hum, and the electric clock on the wall picked up its lost rhythm.

Clay exhaled, and his neck relaxed a smidge. He clicked the remote, but the TV remained dark. "Bet we blew a fuse on that one."

"I'll check, Dad. You sit." Josh headed down the hall to the circuit box, Samson at his heels.

Clay pulled his glasses off and placed them over the arm of his chair. His adrenaline had begun to dissipate, and his arms were dead weight. His eyes itched something terrible, but he suspected that once he closed them, he'd have a hard time getting them open again. He gave in, rubbed them just for a moment, then let his head sink back against the velvety cushion.

The metallic din of trashcans clattering against concrete startled him awake. "Dang coyotes. I'm gonna' put an electric fence around them cans." He strained to see the clock. He'd dozed for about 30 minutes.

No sign of the boy or dog. Must have gone on to bed.

Clay pushed the recliner forward hoping the momentum would help him up. He half-rose, but his legs wobbled, and his knee ached. He sank back into softness. Why fight it? He'd had a full day. Clay pushed the La-Z- Boy back and closed his eyes. Tried to recall what he had burned at supper.

What is that smell? Another sound reached his ears. A car alarm?

Clay squinted. Felt for his glasses. He stopped in mid-reach and cocked his head.

What is that?

His scalp prickled, his mind suddenly alert.

It sounded like a train. No. It sounded like - Oh, Lord - he could smell it.

Clay lunged from the recliner and stumbled into the kitchen.

Over the sink, frenzied orange light ricocheted in through the window.

He flung wide the back door, and the roar of hell itself met him. He launched down the stairs and froze. It seemed the whole earth had stopped.

Flames from the barn surged into the sky while thousands of white ashes floated around him, soft as snowflakes.

• CHAPTER 2 •

Conflagration

"Josh!" Clay screamed, charging through the barn door into the pyre. Fingers of blistering flame stretched down from the hayloft and scorched Clay's face.

Plumes of searing smoke sucked the oxygen from his lungs, dropping him to his knees. His shirt melted into his arms, the metal buttons burning deep into his flesh. He did not notice, and scrambled forward on all fours, the hot pavers peeling layers of skin from his fingers.

The fire roared through what remained of the hayloft, the walls around him pulsed in a feverish mirage. He gasped for air but strangled on the thick smoke, his mouth filling with the coppery taste of blood and panic.

Clay retracted his face into his tee shirt and tumbled forward blind, pressing his left shoulder against the wall.

He knew where the boy would be.

Jubilee's stall. The far end of the barn. Oh God! What was I thinking? Help me find him.

The smoke swirled, parting for a moment to reveal a body in the aisle. Clay rushed forward, eyes straining. His fingers found flesh. And fur.

Samson.

He began an unconscious mantra, "Please don't take him. Don't take him," and crawled faster.

His shaking hand found Jubilee's stall door.

Open.

Clay looked up and saw Josh struggling to open the huge back door of the barn. The sticky door. The one Clay was supposed to have fixed. Behind him, Jubilee reared. Frantic to escape. The door began to move.

Clay's elbow buckled with relief. "Josh!" He screamed, but the fire-roar consumed his voice. He tried to stand but could not seem to get his legs under him. He focused on the floor for a moment, trying to right himself. And somehow he was up. He careened forward, his left hand against the wall.

As the huge door slid sideways, a massive beam in the roof groaned, one end consumed in flame. Chunks of smoldering wood and debris showered onto Clay's head.

The door opened wide enough for a horse to pass.

They were going to escape.

Jubilee reared again, knocking Josh to his knees.

Clay lurched forward. His boy needed help.

Josh struggled to his feet. The other end of the timber broke loose dropping flaming torches of hay. An entire engulfed bale landed on Jubilee's rump, lighting his tail. The horse screamed and leaped over Josh, shooting into the night like a rocket.

The beam floated down in slow motion, slicing through the smoke. It slammed Josh between the shoulder blades pinning him face down inside the doorway of the burning barn.

"NO!" Clay bellowed, clambering forward. He slid to his knees and flung himself, chest-first on the ground, to peer into Josh's green eyes. Oh, those eyes. Evelyn's eyes.

Josh blinked hard and stared back, the whites huge and shocking next to his soot-blackened face.

Clay leaped up, thrust his arms under the beam and tried to move it. Nothing. The behemoth lay across Josh's back, crushing the life from him. It would take three men to lift it. And the fire raged, gaining on them. They didn't have much time.

Josh needed help now!

What could he do? He stood there. Pounded his fists against his temples. He needed to do something now! But what?

Clay's attention darted to the shed. The John Deere, the big one with the hayforks.

He'd blow through the door, get under the beam. Josh would roll out. That would work.

Clay knelt down to explain. "I'm gettin' the tractor." He had to move fast.

"Dad," Josh wheezed.

Clay turned back, "I'm here."

"Don't leave me." The boy sounded tired.

"I'll be right back."

But as Clay skidded into the shed, a sudden coldness traveled up his spine. His hand flew to his throat. He spun around and raced faster than he had run in decades.

His lungs screamed for more oxygen.

More.

His legs couldn't pump fast enough. He threw himself onto his belly next to his boy's still body.

Clay's ragged breath stopped. "Joshie?" He whispered.

But Josh could not answer, his green eyes were fixed, a single tear tracing slowly through the ash on his cheek.

Clay felt his heart implode. Anguish tore through his belly as he writhed on the ground. "Not my boy! Not my Josh." The words spilled out over and over again.

The fire no longer mattered. He would die here, with his boy.

And then the rain came. In huge, distended tears, it poured down from heaven. Like nothing Clay had ever seen.

Clay curled up next to Josh's broken body, his own tears mingling with the mud.

Billy found them the next morning.

• CHAPTER 3 •

Friends

Thirst. Terrible thirst intruded into Clay's oblivion.

Strange sounds. Beeping and far off voices.

And the smell. An acrid, bitter stench of burnt flesh and hair that made his stomach roll. Clay's singed eyebrows twitched, and he worked to focus.

Open.

His lids resisted. Thirst compelled him on.

Cold. So cold.

Clay accomplished a groan. The sound of his own voice made his eyelids flutter.

His tongue grew bolder. "Water." He whispered.

Someone else spoke. Someone far away. Clay could not make out the words, but he heard liquid splash onto ice cubes.

A strong arm supported his back. A straw touched his lips. He clawed at it with his good hand, his arm as shaky as a newborn's. Clay sucked the water into his mouth until the cold dribbled down his chin. The sensation kicked his eyelids open. The strong arm laid him back against a pillow. He blinked against the artificial light in the room.

Confused.

He blinked again, amazed by the difficulty of simply raising and lowering his sandpaper lined lids. He licked his blistered lips and tried to turn his head.

"Where am I?"

"In the hospital, sir."

His memory was blank. "What happened? Where's Josh?"

"We're here, Mr. Westin. Whatever you need." Billy's voice was pity soft.

Eli Jenson echoed from the opposite side of the bed. "Whatever you need Clay. We'll help you get through this."

Get through what?

He is gone.

Josh's face, his beautiful green eyes fixed, slammed Clay's mind. Water, still cool, spewed up from his stomach, soaking the front of Billy's shirt. Clay crumpled, ripping the IV from his arm.

"Nurse!" Billy bellowed. "We need help!"

Billy's yells grew dim. A dark tide washed over Clay, and he welcomed it.

•

"Come on, Mr. Westin, let's change your dressing." The woman's voice sounded young and gentle.

Clay's eyelids flickered. His left hand and both knees throbbed – a compelling toothache-like throb.

The nurse, dressed in green scrubs, unwound the bandage on his hand. She could not have been older than Josh, maybe 21. Her skin was the color of coffee with milk, her large eyes, hazel.

A white lanyard around her neck held her ID card identifying her as Cara.

"Let's see what we've got today," Cara said, addressing his left hand.

"Where am I?" He whimpered, trying to retrieve his arm. Too weak.

She met his eyes, her smile genuinely pleased. "There you are." She returned her attention to his hand. "Welcome back, Mr. Westin. You've been out for a while."

"How long?"

"You were on the burn unit for five days. You have been here two days. We kept you sedated for a while. Seemed best. Your burns are healing well, and your lungs have been clear since yesterday. Dr. Purcell says your heart sounds as good as can be expected."

She spoke in a matter of fact way that made him feel almost calm.

She peeled back the final layer of gauze on his left hand, to reveal the raw meat of a third-degree burn, strangely mingled with irregular white borders against his tan, leathery skin.

"Can you open your hand?"

Clay stretched gingerly. His ring finger was bare. Bile reared up into his throat.

"Where's my ring?" He could hardly whisper.

"We had to cut it off. Your whole hand was badly burned."

"Where is it?"

"With your things."

Clay turned his head toward the wall so she would not see the tears trickle down into the pillow.

"Your friends went to get breakfast," Cara said, slathering ointment in between his fingers. "They've been here day and night. Good friends."

She wrapped his hand in fresh gauze. "TV on?" she asked, brightly.

He rolled the rest of him toward the wall, closed his eyes and tried to will his heart to stop.

•

Eli paced up the hall with Billy towards Clay's new room, his stomach churning. As the pastor of a small town church, he had eaten far too much hospital cafeteria food. But this wasn't just the food.

He could not shake the feeling that Clay had some unfinished business with God. He is a jealous God. The book of

Matthew is clear. "He who loves his son or daughter more than Me is not worthy of Me."

Eli had brought the topic up several times. It wasn't easy talking to a friend about making their son an idol. But God's Word was clear.

No one could say he hadn't tried.

Sometimes Eli wondered if he could shoulder the burden God had entrusted to him. Shepherding even a small church was hard. Eli had held such great expectations for Josh. He sighed. *Such a waste.*

He *was* grateful to be off the burn floor. He would never forget the stench. Burnt hair, charred flesh. Awful.

Cara glanced up as they passed the nurses' station. "He's awake."

Eli and Billy rushed the door at the same time and approached the bed carefully. Clay had curled up on his side facing the wall. He looked even more frail, as though he had shriveled while he and Billy grabbed lunch.

"Clay," Eli whispered. "Are you awake?"

Clay rolled onto his back, his eyes huge and exhausted against his wet, haggard face.

"Why?" Clay breathed, grasping Eli's sleeve.

Eli shook his head. This wasn't the time to share his suspicion. "I don't know." A trickle of frustration rose up, and he tried to push it back down.

"Why would He take my boy – and leave me?"

It's pretty clear to me Clay. But he didn't say it. "I don't know." He fetched a metal folding chair and popped it open next to the bed. "We need to talk about a couple things."

"What things?"

"The funeral for one. You are the only person who can make the arrangements. I've got a form you need to fill out."

"I have to do it now?"

"No, Clay. But soon. You'll need to do it soon."

"Billy," Clay spoke with sudden urgency. "What about Jubilee. Where is he?"

"Don't know, sir. I've looked for him; had a couple other guys look. Don't worry. We'll find him."

Clay signed the burial certificate with Eli's help. Eli backed out of the room, drove the two-hours home, and slept in his own bed for the first time in a week.

Three days later Clay came home from the hospital, and they buried Josh on Saturday. In the family plot, next to his mother, Evelyn. Private ceremony; just Eli, Clay and Billy.

Eli sprinkled dirt onto the casket as he prayed. "The Lord gives; the Lord takes away. Blessed be the name of the Lord."

Clay would not make eye contact. He sat in his wheelchair, shaking.

Eli just shook his head, wondering what it would take for Clay to get it.

•

The next day Eli drove by Clay's house for church. He rang the bell, then knocked. Clay arrived at the front door, disheveled and groggy.

"Aren't you ready?"

"I'm not goin'."

"Come on, Clay. You need to be around other people."

"I'm not goin'. Not today. Not ever."

Eli inhaled so hard he choked on his own spit. *He had waited too long.* "You don't mean it."

Clay glared at him, and Eli felt the desperateness flare in him again. Righteous anger burned deep in his soul. *Who did Clay think he was? To tell God His business? More wrath would surely follow.*

"If I were you, Clay, I'd fall on my knees and beg God for mercy. He's trying to teach you something. This is not the time to close your ears."

But Clay closed the door on Eli's face and went back to bed.

• CHAPTER 4 •

Memories

One Year Later

Clay hunched down to pick up a handful of earth. He broke through the grainy crust and gathered the soil into his hand, crumbling it between stiff fingers.

Drought had reduced the ranch to dust. The dirt felt like everything else in Clay's life. Dead. Dry.

Josh's horse. You promised.

The thought sounded so clear, so real, Clay shook his head and answered out loud. "I can't."

He'll die out there, and it will be your fault. Like everything else.

A dust-devil whipped up and cavorted around him, first stealing the loam as it slipped from between his fingers, then strafing his arms and face with tiny sand bullets. The skin on his left hand and forearm was still paper thin and pink. He covered it gently with his other.

Clay's weary eyes followed the whirlwind as it spun past the burned-out barn, past the silent stone house, past the neglected paddocks and beyond, into acres and acres of dryness. A rustling sound caught his ear, and he froze. His blood surged.

Jubilee?

It was just the rattle of dead mesquite bushes, scourged by the wind.

You've done nothing. You are nothing.

He pressed his thumb and forefinger into his eyes. His lungs wanted a deep breath, but he didn't have the energy. He turned and shuffled toward the empty house.

The can of pork and beans nearly bested him. Twice the can opener slipped off the lip of the can. The second time he caught his thumb on the jagged edge of the exposed lid, ripping it open in a small triangle, deep into the pad where the swirl of fingerprint lay. It burned like snakebite. "Dang it!"

Serves you right.

He squeezed the torn thumb until it turned white, started the faucet with his elbow and watched his blood mix with water and trickle down the drain.

The physical pain distracted momentarily from the silent roar in his soul, and he squeezed tighter. He band-aided the thumb and snatched a plastic spoon from the box. He headed for his worn recliner in the great-room, eating the beans cold, straight from the can.

The TV blared 24/7 most days. It gave an illusion of life.

Jeopardy concluded, and he rubbed at the tightness in the back of his neck grasping for a sensation of drowsiness.

Sleep sometimes offered a respite from the thoughts.

He tossed the empty can into an overfull trash bag and trudged down the hall, working his tongue over his palate to scrape away the waxy feeling from supper.

Framed photos of his family lined the walls from the living room to the bedroom.

His daily gauntlet.

His mother's words rolled across his memory.

It's better to have loved and lost.

"You were wrong, Mom." Clay stared at Pearl's grainy, yellowed portrait. Without it, he'd have been unable to recall her face, except her eyes. He couldn't forget her eyes. He saw them every time he looked in the mirror. Tired, like old denim. Empty.

The other images were all Evelyn or Josh or the horses. He'd thought about taking the pictures down a million times but couldn't imagine what he would do next. Pack 'em in a box, like they never existed? And to get them in the box, he'd have to look at them. Remember.

Like that one. Josh's graduation from Texas A&M, with Clay beaming up at his boy. Josh, all six feet of him, grinning in his goofy way, holding his fingers in rabbit ears over Clay's head.

And next to it, the one of Josh and Jubilee. The colt, three weeks old, laying across Josh's long legs as the two dozed under the oak trees in the near pasture. *Oh, God, help me,* he pleaded.

The photos became a battering ram against his soul. He pushed his chin upwards and pursed his lips, creating a sort of dam. The question shoved its way through anyhow.

Why? Why? Why?

His heart shifted, his emotions began to unglue. The tenuous edge of reason he continuously balanced began to quake. He turned away from the wall before he lost himself in the memory. If he started, he'd never stop. The abyss would swallow him.

Just keep goin'. Make it to the bedroom.

Clay perched on the edge of his unmade bed slipped his boots off and climbed in. He pulled a grimy sheet over him, dusty jeans and all. He leaned against the headboard and picked up one of his prescription bottles.

Westin, Clay. Lasix. One tablet once a day, for cardiac failure. Heart failure. Didn't need a doctor to tell him that.

What if I stopped taking the pills?

He couldn't. He could see himself drowning inside his own lungs, flopping, gasping, desperate for air - like a fish on a rock. *And then*?

Clay quickly placed the tablet in his mouth and bit the edge of his tongue to gather enough saliva to swallow.

Coward.

He glanced at the clock. 8:20. His gaze stopped at the Bible, dusty and untouched on the nightstand. He hadn't read it since that night.

God doesn't care about you .

I know.

But his arm reached over and picked up the leather-bound book. He stretched his hand across the rough surface smoothing a layer of dust from the cover.

His fingers touched the letters engraved on the lower right corner. Clay David Westin.

He pulled his knees up and cradled the book in the bend of his body. He caressed the letters with his fingertips. The gold had long ago worn off most of them, but bumps from the raised edges remained. *Like Braille,* he mused, as he closed his eyes and felt the letters a third time.

Suddenly a need to remember her became stronger than the need to forget and he lifted back the cover.

Slowly.

He opened his eyes. Evelyn's handwriting was small and neat, just as she had been. He turned to the Weddings page.

> To Clay David. I will always love you.
> Evelyn Mayfield. October 14, 1944.

He ran the tips of his fingers over those letters longing to feel them, to feel her, or something from her just once more.

He turned to the next page. The Births page. Written in his own untidy hand.

Joshua Noel Westin. Born December 25, 1970.

He leaned his head back against the wall and remembered the morning she told him.

May 29, 1970

Clay studied the mare. Her milk-bag had shrunk, and she looked less likely to foal anytime soon. "Gettin' too old to sleep in the barn," he muttered, rocking his head side to side to loosen the crick in his neck.

Might be time to hire someone younger to help with foaling season. He headed toward the house. The driveway was empty; Evie had already gone into town.

Coffee. The earthy fragrance lured him to the kitchen. He couldn't wait to get some. Evie had placed the paper on the counter where he'd surely see it. He poured a cup and glanced at the headlines.

Clay held the mug to his lips touching the rounded edge tentatively. He slurped a tiny amount. Strong. The way he liked it. He allowed the brew to warm his mouth for a moment before swallowing.

The front door slam stopped his reading. Evie, home from her errands. She must be feeling better. He could hear it in the lightness of her footsteps.

He spun around to watch her walk through the kitchen door. He was always surprised by the thrill that overtook him when their eyes met.

Twenty-six years of marriage and the sight of her still made his face warm.

She rushed through the doorway but stopped short when their eyes met. She had been half-smiling, but when she saw him, her cheeks dimpled, and her eyes sparkled. Those eyes. He was helplessly lost inside of them. He never wanted to be anywhere else.

Evie cocked her head with her what-am-I-going-to-do-with-you look. "Clay, honey, you're exhausted. Sit down; let me rub your shoulders." She plopped her keys and bulging grocery bag on the counter.

He obeyed quickly, pulling a chair from the kitchen table. He rolled his head and shrugged, inviting her touch. She always knew where he was tight.

"How are you feeling?" he murmured, pressing the back of his head against her belly.

She giggled and danced around him, pirouetting before she dropped, breathless in his lap. She threw her arms around his neck and leaned back, her smile full of news.

He could only stare, open-mouthed. "Evelyn. What's gotten into you?"

She tossed her red hair, now sprinkled with gray, and caressed his face. Clay covered her hand with his own, holding her cool palm against his cheek. She gazed into him with an intensity that made his heart thud.

"What is it?" he whispered, fear tingling in the back of his throat.

"Clay Westin, you are going to be a daddy!" She leaped up, eyes shining.

"What?" The chair tipped dangerously. He barely caught himself.

"We're having a baby. I saw Doc Phillips this morning."

"Why, why'd you do that?"

"I had a feeling." Her voice grew soft as she placed her hand over her abdomen. "I needed to know."

"Aren't you...you know?" A remnant of his senses returned, and he thought better of the question. "Aren't we too old?"

"Silly," she gushed. "Charlie Chaplin had a baby when he was 73."

He rolled his eyes. "Evelyn, his wife had the baby. She was younger than he was. We are in our forties. Our friends are havin' grand-babies."

She bent and pressed her forehead against his. "Oh, Clay," she said, in almost a whisper, "this is a miracle. An answer to prayer." She stood, and her voice grew. "It's just a little later than we'd planned. God's plan is always better."

"I know. But..."

She came around behind him and continued the massage. "And our baby is due around Christmas. What do you think about Joshua Noel?"

"It's good."

She gave that spot on his neck one last thumb press. "I've got to get the pork chops put away."

"Joshua Noel," he whispered. "How do you know it's a boy?"

Evelyn popped her head up over the fridge door. "I just know."

Clay became aware that he'd clenched his fists tight. He opened his fingers slowly, painfully. He rubbed them against his jeans, then counted the months. Seven more to go.

"A baby. A daddy. I'm a daddy." The word felt precious on his tongue. He said it over and over. "Daddy."

Clay licked his finger, closed his eyes, and turned the fragile gilded page. The next page of the Bible.

The Deaths page.

Evelyn Mayfield Westin. December 25, 1970.

He could still *see* the moment when Dr. Rice called him from the waiting room, spectacles spattered with blood. Clay closed his eyes and went there again.

Christmas Eve, 1970

Evie stopped stirring the soup and rubbed her protruding belly. She gazed around the warm kitchen, eyebrows knitted together in deep thought. She seemed far away. Clay had seen that look before. In mares right before they foaled.

"You alright?" Clay jumped to his feet.

"It's nothing," she insisted, "I just wrapped too many presents."

"Let's go ahead into the hospital," he said, in his desperate voice, the one she usually heeded.

"I'm fine, Clay. Quit fussing over me," she huffed. She turned the burner down to simmer and gave him a quick smile. "I'm not finished yet. I want the house ready when we come home with him."

He lay awake all night, listening to her breathe. At 3:00 AM, he felt her body tighten as the first hard pains began. She rolled over, grunting with the effort, and turned her face to his, "It's time, let's go."

"Thank God," he whispered, springing from the bed to help her dress. He grabbed the navy overcoat from the closet and placed it gently on her shoulders. Her hand gripped his, and they walked.

He tossed her bag in the truck. The dark, cool air braced him, and he drank in a deep breath.

The truck roared to life, and as Clay shifted, he noticed beads of perspiration on her upper lip. Her nostrils flared, and she arched back against the leather seat. She moaned softly and shifted her weight.

"Hang on, Evie," he cried. He gunned the motor, sending up a spray of gravel. Why didn't I find an apartment close to the hospital?

"I'm okay," she blew out through her lips. "Just think, this time tomorrow we'll have our boy." She breathed in. "Don't worry Clay. Women have been having babies for a long time."

"I know." He pushed the pedal even harder and prayed silently. I know.

Clay screeched into the ambulance entrance of the emergency room. "Help!" he yelled. "My wife needs help!"

Two nurses appeared with a wheelchair and whisked Evie away. She waved goodbye over her head. He lifted his hand to wave back, even though he knew she couldn't see.

He parked the truck and stood for a moment at the front desk feeling lost and relieved at the same time. A heavy-set nurse with too much blue eyeshadow shot him a tired twitch of a smile and handed him a clipboard.

He stood at the desk, filled out the paperwork and waited, unsure what to do next. The nurse scanned the pages, stopping for a moment at Evie's age. She stared from under her blue eyelids. "Kind of late to start a family."

A shrug was all he could manage. He retreated to the waiting room. Now, all he had to do was wait.

"Mr. Westin."

He'd fallen asleep in the chair. "Here," he said, jerking his hand in the air just like in that math class after lunch in - was that sixth grade?

But the voice belonged to Dr. Rice. He stood over Clay's chair, his watery eyes red-rimmed and exhausted. A delicate spray of dried blood decorated his bifocals. Clay couldn't take his eyes off the blood.

"Mr. Westin, can you come with me please?" Dr. Rice's voice stretched out in a careful monotone.

The room shrank in an instant. Clay couldn't feel his legs. The edges around his peripheral vision grew dark until all he saw was the spray on Dr. Rice's glasses. He wasn't certain how he became upright.

Dr. Rice stared at the floor. His head snatched up to make momentary eye contact. "This way," he held out his arm as a guide. They walked slowly, side by side, down the dim institution yellow hallway.

"Mr. Westin ... I," Dr. Rice increased his stride. "I..."

Clay watched his own feet. He couldn't feel them, but they obviously worked. His gaze moved to the pea green linoleum squares, and then to the black dress shoes beside his own. Why would anyone choose pea green linoleum?

"Mr. Westin," the feet stopped. "You have a son." Dr. Rice did not sound happy.

Clay looked up. They stood outside the double doors of the delivery room. Dr. Rice cleared his throat and pressed his lips together. "Your wife had a condition called Placenta Previa. The placenta covers the cervix and causes uncontrollable bleeding during delivery. We tried to perform a Caesarean Section but - well, we did everything we could. I am sorry. We were able to save your son."

What do you mean? Clay wanted to shout. He opened his mouth, but his tongue betrayed him. Here, in the most important moment of his life, it had gone numb. He watched Dr. Rice's mouth. Surely something, something else would be said?

My sweet Evie. Gone? His mind would not accept it. It was not possible.

Dr. Rice reached forward to push the heavy door to the delivery room.

Clay stumbled forward into the harsh glare of the overhead lights. He leaned against the wall, dizzy and disoriented. He stared about the room, searching for her. A hamper stuffed with crimson soaked sheets and gauze stood in one corner. The sharp scent of blood mingled with anesthesia made his stomach flutter.

Evie lay on a steel surgical bed in the opposite corner, a sheet up to her chin. Her eyes were almost closed. A pan on the floor caught the scarlet trickle as it dripped rhythmically from the corner of the gurney.

Her face looked so peaceful that if Clay had passed by quickly or if he hadn't known her, he might have thought she was sleeping. But he wasn't passing quickly, and he did know her, and his heart understood the moment he saw her. She was really gone.

A long, thin, keening sound he did not recognize came from his mouth. His legs buckled and he hit the floor knees first. He was vaguely aware of people scooping him up under the armpits and placing him in a rocking chair.

He curled his fist against his mouth, crushing his knuckles into his lips until they both bled. He could not pull his eyes from Evie's face.

A young black nurse moved in front of him, blocking his view of the body. She carried a bundle against her chest and bent low. "Sir. Mr. Westin." She opened one arm toward him so he could see. "Would you like to hold your son?"

Her calm, clear voice compelled Clay's attention. He could only nod.

The nurse smiled and placed the bundle into his lap, waiting until he could get his arms under and around it. She stayed for a moment, arms extended, as though he might drop the baby, then pulled another chair next to him.

Clay folded his elbows in, drawing the infant to himself. His trembling fingers peeled back the blanket, and he found himself staring into Evelyn's green eyes. He glanced at the nurse. She nodded, and he pushed back the tiny cap. Red hair.

A whimper slipped from his lips. He hated that. Didn't want his first word to be incoherent. Clay cradled Joshua Noel into the space between his shoulder and cheek and breathed in the sweetness of newborn baby. His baby. Evie's baby.

He allowed the tears to roll unimpeded, as he rocked. Clay blinked at the nurse, "I'm sorry. It's just ... he looks so much like her."

"He's beautiful sir. Most beautiful baby I've ever seen." Her eyes glistened as she rubbed Clay's arm. His shoulders began to ache, and he relaxed them, bringing Josh onto his lap, and back into view. His heart throbbed with adoration so fierce it made him dizzy.

"Mr. Westin, my name is Kristine. I'm here to help you with your son." She perched forward on her chair. Her presence helped him, focused him.`

"Thank you," he managed to whisper. He gazed into Josh's eyes again as purpose enveloped him and he could breathe.

Joshua's tiny tongue peeked from between his perfect heart shaped lips.

"Here is a bottle. I think he's hungry." Kristine showed him how to hold the bottle, so Josh did not get air in his little belly. It was just the same as nursing a foal really.

The infant grasped Clay's finger in his fist as he suckled. Clay rocked gently. They stayed that way, the two of them, for a long while, gazing at each other.

When Clay looked up, they had wheeled Evie's body away.

The Bible slid from Clay's lap and landed with a soft thump on the floor. "Oh, God. Why would you take them?" His cry echoed into the emptiness of the house.

He heard no answer, and his body writhed involuntarily into his pre-born shape on the filthy bed.

• CHAPTER 5 •

Invitation

Someone pounded on the front door. Insistent. Rude.

Clay's eyes would not open. He felt drugged, weak, almost liquid. He fought to raise his eyelids. He glanced at the clock. Nine. He couldn't remember the last time he'd slept 'til nine.

Now the discordant chime of the doorbell. *Eli. Why won't he leave me alone?*

Clay struggled with the sheet and stumbled towards the door. He stopped at the window in the front hall, pushed down one slat of the blinds. No car. Couldn't be Eli. Unless he'd hidden it around back. He checked the mirror and ran his fingers over his wispy hair. He needed a haircut.

"I'm comin'," he snapped. He cracked the door just enough

to peer out.

"Mr. Westin?" Unfamiliar male voice. Young.

Clay found himself staring directly into the sun. "Who's there?" He brought his hand up to shade his eyes and stepped back into the comfort of his cool dark foyer. The stranger followed him in.

Clay was blind. Totally blind. Light flooded in, filling the room.

"Who's there?" Clay wanted to sound authoritative, but his voice squeaked like a pubescent boy. *He had to get that door closed. Couldn't see anything.* He tried to clear his throat, but the dang phlegm wouldn't budge.

"Hello, Mr. Westin, my name is Gabe. I've come to check on you, sir. See if there's anything you need."

"No, no." Clay shook his head. "Doin' just fine." He squeezed his eyes hard. The spots were clearing. His vision had almost returned.

"What's your name son? Did Eli send you?" Clay didn't bother to keep the edge from his voice.

The young man did not seem to notice and extended his hand. "My name is Gabe sir. I'm a friend of Josh."

Clay studied the young man's smooth face. Gabe's earnest brown eyes were guileless. He looked about 23, same age Josh ... *would have been.*

His easy smile held no trace of sarcasm, his cheeks still had boyish roundness to them, but he had the physique of a lifeguard. Strong.

Made Clay feel even less sociable.

"You heard what happened here?"

"Yes, sir. A year ago today. I'm so sorry for your pain."

Clay's heart fluttered, and he fell backward against the wall. He clapped his hand over his chest trying to draw a breath, but the air felt thick, like smoke.

"Are you all right?" Gabe stepped forward, grasping Clay by the elbow.

"I'm... I can't believe it's been a year."

Clay staggered toward the bench in the hallway. He sat quickly before he could fall. *A year?*

What if I had gone? I should have left that big door open. What if I'd put Jube in the front stall? Like I should have. I should have. This should be Josh answering the door. Not me.

He closed his eyes and rocked, rubbing his palms hard

against his thighs. Would he ever think of anything else? Ever? Forever.

He sat for several moments, the word forever rattling about in his soul.

He opened his eyes mildly surprised to see the young man still standing there. He'd forgotten about him.

The boy stared at him. Expectantly.

Clay's right ear suddenly itched something terrible, and he busied himself for moments as he waited for the young man to do something.

Leave.

Talk.

Something.

Clay scrutinized the slate floor for several minutes before flopping his hands onto his knees and staring pointedly at the front door.

The young man did not take the hint but kept his eyes on Clay. He was like a Golden Retriever puppy. Too happy-natured to know when someone was just plain miserable.

Clay exhaled surrender loudly, "I was just gonna' have some breakfast. Care to join me?"

"Love to," Gabe answered, extending his hand to help Clay rise. "What are you having?"

"Shredded Wheat, if the milk's not bad."

Milk passed the sniff test. They ate the cereal from Styrofoam bowls.

Gabe gazed around the spacious kitchen. "Your house is amazing, Mr. Westin."

"Thank you, young man." Clay contemplated the wheat biscuit on his spoon. He didn't feel irritated anymore. Just tired. "You know; you spend your whole life gettin' ready for somethin'. Somethin' you don't even know you're gettin' ready for. And then one day you realize." He put the spoon down before it dropped. "I spent my life tryin' to make sure Josh's life was better than mine."

A small whiny sound escaped, and he pressed his fist against his lips. *Hold it together.*

"Mr. Westin. Are you sure I can't help you do something? Anything?" Gabe's curly brown hair fell forward, and he pushed it back, his eyes gleaming with sincerity.

So young. So eager. So much like my Josh.

Clay shook his head. "No. I'll be fine."

Jubilee, the voice nudged.

A strange, disembodied sensation swept over Clay. The intense wave of grief subsided, and he could suddenly breathe. "I need to find Josh's horse," he heard himself say. "He's been running loose on my ranch." He felt like someone else was speaking - or like he was watching himself speak.

"Sir, I'd like to help you. I've got a couple good horses and a pack mule."

Clay shook his head to re-orient himself. "What? You want to help me? I've got 30,000 acres. It could take days...weeks. Or longer." Just thinking about the expanse made him deflate. "I've already sent three search parties. Nobody's even seen a hoof print."

"I would be honored to help you." Gabe's face shone.

It was a crazy notion. Clay debated the idea while taking a quick physical inventory. He'd actually slept for several hours - that was good. He'd eaten breakfast today *and* dinner the night before. "I don't have a horse," Clay realized out loud.

"That's OK. I've got a gray mare. You two will get along fine."

The young man's enthusiasm woke a hopefulness Clay had

not allowed himself in a long while. Adrenaline coursed through his veins. “Let’s do it!” He crowed, feeling more alive than he had in years.

Gabe grinned. “Let’s go!”

“Your horses are here?”

“Yessir. Out back.”

Clay shook his head in disbelief. He stood up and knocked the chair over. “I need to pack.” He rushed to his room, snatched a bag from the closet floor and stuffed it with a couple pairs of socks and underwear. He changed his jeans, grabbed his heart meds and headed down the hall.

The photo of Josh with Jubilee stopped him again. He took it from the wall with trembling hands. “I’ll bring him back Joshie. I’ll make him whole. I promise.” His chin quivered as he replaced the picture.

Clay’s excitement rose. He could hear the horses. The snorting, stamping, wonderful sounds of horses. Clay snagged his hat, took a deep breath, opened the back door and stepped into the warm sun.

• CHAPTER 6 •

Selel

Standing behind Gabe's mule stood a silver mare who turned her head and nickered right into Clay. His face went tight and buzzy, and he staggered forward into Gabe.

"Whoa, sir. Are you all right?" Gabe clutched Clay's good arm at the elbow, his eyes searching.

But Clay could not take his eyes from the mare. He grappled with Gabe's arm, trying to find his balance. He teetered momentarily, his mouth opening and closing like a fish. He couldn't get his mouth around a single word.

He thumped his chest and stumbled forward. "What's her name?" It sounded more like a puff of air, but somehow Gabe heard.

"Selel."

"That's a strange name," Clay said without taking his gaze from the gray.

The mare watched him approach, her soft eyes luminous.

"It's Hebrew," Gabe said, his voice real soft.

That's right. He was friends with Josh. Of course, he would name his horse something in Hebrew.

Selel stepped forward to meet him and placed her head against Clay's chest. She didn't push, she simply stood, eyes closed.

His eyes burned, and he rubbed them with the back of his hand. "This horse ... this horse is the spittin' image of a mare I used to have."

"Tell me about your mare."

"No son." Clay ran his hand down the front of Selel's face feeling her delicate facial bones. "It was a long time ago."

He moved toward the saddle, stopped, pressed his face into her neck and inhaled. She smelled good, like sweat and grass and honesty. Horses. They had been his life. Once.

He stepped back and tried to bring his foot up high enough to reach the stirrup. Not even close.

"May I help you, Sir?"

"Dang it."

Weakling.

Clay sighed with an ache that seemed to ooze from the marrow of his bones. "Yeah, I guess I need help."

Gabe laced his fingers together and hoisted Clay into the saddle. Clay settled his feet into the stirrups while Selel curved her neck around and snuffled the tip of his boot. He reached down and rubbed her neck. Like they'd been together forever.

Gabe mounted his Paint and waited. "Where to, sir?"

Clay rolled the reins into his good hand and pointed his body to the north. "The lake." That's where Jubilee would be. "Only place with any water."

His body remembered the rhythm of the ride. Each hoof-step begun before the last ended. He felt Selel's body under his, the power in her shoulders, heartbeat pulsing through the saddle.

He'd missed the magic of the ebb and flow of muscles, tendons, sinew moving in harmony. It was like electricity. An unseen powerful connection. He closed his eyes and felt her, moved with her, and before he could think to push it down, Shadow's memory surged up.

He could not resist. He would not.

His heart and mind returned to a cool April morning, more than 60 years in the past.

April 17, 1933

Clay tiptoed barefoot through the wet grass toward the barn. It was early, too early for the sun. The light in the barn could mean only one thing. Trouble or a foal. At seven years old he could only dream of helping.

He peeked around the stall door. "Can I help you?" He hated that his voice came out high and quavery. Clay was never sure what to call his father. Dad seemed too close, Father too formal. He usually just avoided.

Milton jerked his head up - surprised. He lay on his left side, up to his shoulder in a black broodmare. "Where's Eric? Why ain't you in bed?" His words erupted in between grunts of pain as the mare's contractions crushed his arm.

Clay slipped through the door into the stall. "I saw the light in the barn. I want to help."

His father pulled his arm slowly from Midnight's body and sat up. "You want to help, go get Eric."

Clay's shoulders fell forward, and he turned to comply.

"Wait. C'mon back here. Even you should be able to do this."

Clay lurched forward, unable to believe his luck. He got his feet under him and walked carefully around the prone mare, his stomach whirling.

"Looky here. Hold the foot. That's all. Just hold the foot." His father looked bleary-eyed and spent. Clay smelled alcohol on his breath, as usual.

Clay grasped the pastern joint, just above the tiny cone-shaped hoof. He knew he should look away, but his eyes were drawn to the miniature paisley shaped nostrils peeking from the placental shroud under Midnight's tail.

"I'm gettin' rope. You hang on to that foot, hear?"

Clay nodded without looking up. He would not lose the foot.

His father returned, and Clay moved aside. He watched his father fix a square-knot around the fragile pastern joint and pull. "C'mon mare," he groaned, the veins in his neck bulging.

Midnight made a sound Clay had never heard from a horse. It was a pitiful noise – sounded like an inhaled scream.

"That's it," Milton ceased pulling and handed Clay the rope. "I'm gonna' lose my best mare if we keep up. I'll have to cut it out. It's prob'ly dead anyway. She's been pushing too long."

"Cut it out?" Clay swallowed. "How?"

"With a wire. You hold that foot. I'll be back."

Midnight moaned, straining again. Clay watched a powerful contraction ripple across her belly and hated the helpless feeling that gathered in his own. Without warning, Midnight's body sucked the foal back in. "Oh, God! Help me," Clay breathed. "If Dad comes back and I've lost the foot he'll kill me."

Clay held his breath and plunged one hand into Midnight. Slippery warmth enveloped his arm, and he pushed on. He found the forward foot with the rope, then the face.

Clay poked his thumb into the mouth by accident and was shocked to feel a tongue curl around his thumb. He struggled for a handhold and found a second foot bent way back.

Oh, Lord, he would need two hands. He closed his eyes and reached in. He pulled, but the foal seemed stuck on a ledge of some sort. He had a forward leg and a stuck leg.

The contraction passed, and the mare drew in a shuddering breath. Clay relaxed and felt Midnight's body start to push again.

Clay waited.

Midnight's body propelled his arms upwards and to the right. As he rotated both hooves in that direction, he felt a click and a release. And then he had two feet and no resistance. Clay pulled, gently, terrified of hurting the mare or foal further.

But Midnight exhaled like a train, gathered herself and gave a Herculean push. Her legs went rigid, muscles spasming. The foal's ears emerged.

Clay put his back into it. Pulled as hard as he could and in one slippery, waterlogged moment, Clay had the entire baby in his lap.

Amniotic fluid slopped from the torn placenta, baptizing him with sticky broth. The barn filled with the sickening sweet smell of birth.

Clay gathered the tiny horse and scooted back out of the way. The thick umbilical cord still throbbed blue-red with life and prevented him from moving too far.

His hands shook as he stripped off the rest of the birth sack and gazed at the foal, soaked and limp as a rag-doll. He pulled a handful of straw and began rubbing as he stole a quick glance between the hind legs.

"You're a girl," he whispered as he worked.

The foal lay still a moment more, then popped up onto her sternum. She wrinkled her tiny nose and sneezed. Her body trembled as she thrust her shiny muzzle into Clay's hands, little pink tongue protruding.

Clay's father rounded the corner, wires dangling from his fists. "What the ... what did you do?" his voice high pitched with irritation.

"I ... I don't know," Clay stuttered. "I just pulled to one side and next thing I know, there's a foal in my lap."

"Stop messin' with it. Get it up to the mare."

But Midnight hadn't moved. Clay's father lifted her tail. "Dang it. I think she's bleedin' out."

"Wha'does that mean?"

"See the blood, Clay. Life's in the blood. That's her life goin' into the straw." He flung the wire into the straw. "Dang."

Clay watched the scarlet torrent pulsing from Midnight's still body.

"Don't go and get yourself attached to that foal Clay. I'm gonna' have ta shoot it," Milton warned, shaking his head.

Clay placed his arms protectively around the filly's tiny neck. "No. Why?"

"Its mama is dyin'. I don't have time to nurse an orphan. It'll starve to death."

"I'll take care of her! I can do it!" Tears rolled down his cheeks unnoticed.

"What are you gonna' feed it?"

"I'll milk the goat."

"You'll have to go ask yer ma about the goat," Milton shrugged. "If she says you can, come back and we'll see if we can get somethin' from Midnight before she dies. It'll be easier if you can get some first milk into the foal. It's a ton a work Clay. Foal will likely die." He narrowed his eyes. "Are you sure you're up to it?"

Milton's dark eyes traveled back to the mare and Clay could see he was reconsidering.

Clay nodded vigorously. "I'm sure. I'm sure I can do it." He raced to find Mama.

"Mama!" he shrieked, his call punctuated by the slam of the screen door.

She jumped and spun around, hand over her heart, eyebrows high. "What?"

Midnight had a foal, a filly ... but she's dyin'."

Mama's body relaxed slightly. "Who's dying? The filly?"

"No. Midnight. She's bleedin' to death." He felt a twinge of sorrow, quickly replaced by proprietary excitement. His own foal.

Clay's mother released her pent-up breath. "I'm sorry Clay, I know she was your favorite."

"Dad said I could raise her foal ... if you would let me have milk from one of the goats."

Ma squinted, looking puzzled. "Why would he say that? I've only got one milker. The others are feeding their babies."

"I don't need milk. I'll drink water."

"I don't want you drinking water. You're a growing boy. You need your milk." She sighed, wiping her soap reddened hands on her apron. "I'll see what I can figure out."

"I need it soon. She's gonna' wake up, and she'll be hungry."

"You go on Clay. I'll get you some milk."

Milton tied Midnight's legs back so she wouldn't kick. There was no need. She slipped away as quietly as the tears from Clay's eyes. He milked Midnight until her still body yielded no more.

"I'll take care of your baby," he promised the dying mare.

Clay rigged a bottle from his father's calving supplies and sat cross-legged in the straw, the baby in his lap. The filly nursed eagerly, pulling every drop from the bottle. The colostrum seemed to strengthen the foal, and she threw her long legs out in front of her. He rubbed her neck, and she leaned into him like a cat, using his hand for balance.

She managed to stand, but momentum carried her right back down again. She tried once more, lurched forward and scrambled sideways. Each step, exaggerated as she began to make sense of her muscles and forces of gravity. She gained some control over her long legs and ceased all movement.

The filly's knees began to shake, and she leaned against Clay for support. Her back just reached his waist. He stepped aside, and the foal collapsed in a flaccid heap.

"Tuckered you out, I guess," he smiled, settling himself in the straw. He could not keep his hands off of her. Clay curled her tiny forelock around his finger, then caressed her delicate ear. Her coat, wavy with dampness, was black, like her mama's and he ran his fingers through the soft ringlets. A couple of white hairs stood out around her muzzle and eyes.

"Here Clay," his mother opened the stall door and handed him a full bottle, frothy and warm.

"Thank you, Ma,"

"You're welcome." She folded her arms and leaned back against the wall watching the filly nurse.

Clay looked up. "Why you cryin'?"

She flicked the tear with her finger. "No reason."

She turned to head back to the house. "I hope she does right by you."

Selel hopped over a fallen sapling nearly unseating Clay and definitely interrupting his remembering. He automatically tucked his hips and pushed against the horn of the saddle for balance.

"How much farther?" Gabe yelled from behind.

"Not much," Clay answered, hoping he was right. The trail looked very different from the last time he'd ridden it.

Selel began blowing out through her nose, then Gabe's mule started. Clay smelled it too. Something dead.

Clay urged Selel faster, his heart throbbing in his chest. He was too late. He knew it. He knew it. He knew it.

• CHAPTER 7 •

Father's House

They cantered up over the rise and could see the lake. Or what had been the lake. It was now a vast mud pit.

Acres of fish and turtle carcasses littered the area. Dozens of vultures had ventured into the ooze too soon and been trapped in the sticky muck.

They laid with their wings outspread, waiting for death. Hundreds more squabbled on the shoreline waiting for the mud to dry enough to bear their weight.

As the horses drew near, the birds boiled upwards, a heavy, evil-looking cloud. They flapped massive wings, sending their strange pungent odor towards Clay in musty waves. He closed his eyes and averted his head. "Oh, God," he whispered. "Where is Jubilee?"

"Over here, sir," Gabe yelled. "Hoofprints."

Clay clucked Selel into a canter.

"He's heading north," Clay breathed. "Straight to Hell." He felt his tiny bit of strength evaporate.

"Where?"

"My father's house," Clay answered softly, covering his eyes with his hand. He rubbed his pounding temples.

Gabe shaded his eyes as he gazed northward. "Yea, though I walk through the valley of the shadow of death, I will fear no evil: For You are with me. Thy rod and Thy staff, they comfort me."

"Great comfort," Clay said, his lip tightening into a snarl. "My dad used to say 'spare the rod, spoil the child.' He didn't spare it. He used it on everyone."

"I'm sorry sir. That must have been terrible."

"It was a ..." Clay muttered. Swallowed hard. "I swore I would never go back. It's straight ahead, about a mile. Where the tracks are heading."

"Ah," Gabe nodded.

"Dang it! Why would Jube go there? It's the only place on this whole ranch I *can't* go."

"When were you there last?"

"After I married Evie, almost fifty years ago." *Fifty years? It didn't seem possible.* "The last time I was there we buried my father."

You killed him.

"How did your dad die?"

Clay snapped his head around and glared at the young man. *Who did he think he was? What business did he have asking that?* He restrained himself. "I don't want to talk about it. Some things are better left alone, in the past, where they belong."

"Yes sir," Gabe nodded.

They continued up the trail, without talking. Clay's lungs felt tight and brittle, like sudden pneumonia. He tried a quick breath but could not suck in hard enough to pull the air past his closed throat. *Suffocating. I can't breathe.*

Sissy.

Clay's anger flared. He gripped it. Embraced it. It was the only way he would survive. Panic would consume him otherwise. *I hate you. I hate the things you did. To Mama, to me, to the horses.*

Crybaby.

I won't cry. He stuffed the emotions down, packing them in. He felt them jumble together. Confused. Anger or hurt? Heartbreak or terror? They blended into a quiet rage. That was safe. He could control that. Anger didn't make him cry. It made him strong. *Masculine.*

A muscle in his right eyelid began twitching rhythmically. He rubbed the offending eye. It did no good.

The dull headache he had lived with for the past year started pulsing. It crept up the back of his neck like a centipede and continued over the top of his skull before settling in just behind his eyes. It had taken a break for the day. He hadn't noticed its absence until its return.

Clay squirmed in the saddle. His butt hurt and stomach acid slid up his throat burning the back of his mouth. *Forgot the Tums*, he realized. He tried to gather enough spit to swallow. Needed to swallow hard enough to make the acid stay down.

He felt the past pulling at him ... sucking him in... refusing to be suppressed any longer.

It doesn't matter. What is left of me?

Nothing.

Selel picked up the pace.

Clay's hands shook. He looped the reins over the horn of the saddle and rubbed his jaw. He had to stop clenching his teeth. He was going to shatter one of his crowns.

We should be there. Where is it?

Selel trotted around a curve in the trail into a clearing. And there it stood.

Fifty years of decay had turned the tired little farmhouse into a hovel. Sheets of rusty roof metal had peeled back to reveal rotting cross supports.

Wild roses reached thorny arms through shattered windows. A few dry scabs of white paint remained in protected areas while the exposed boards looked like gray bones.

Clay lurched from the saddle, nearly toppling in the process. Gabe stood at his elbow to steady him.

"Get away from me!" Clay barked. "I can get off a horse without help."

Gabe nodded, backing up.

Clay dropped the reins. This house, this hated house, only looked pathetic. Clay's anger flared. *What did I expect?*

I wanted to throw rocks at the windows, he realized. *To break something.*

Stupid. You can't hurt a house .

It's not the house I want to hurt.

Clay stared into the corner of the house. An ancient pecan tree, hollow with disease had fallen, taking out part of the stone chimney. "I wish that tree had fallen on my room when *I* was in it," he muttered.

There would have been no Josh.

Clay brushed the thought away with his hand as he staggered to the back porch. It was only part of the house still intact. That and the cornerstones. The corners and the porch were built upon fieldstones he and Eric had found.

Eric again. *I haven't thought of Eric in years.*

His anger evaporated as he melted onto the step. The stones felt warm on his seat.

"I don't know what I expected to see," he mumbled. "I thought it would look the same. Stupid huh?"

"What happened here, Sir?" Gabe asked.

"Too much," Clay replied shaking his head and motioning Gabe away. He had to stop thinking, remembering. He squeezed his mouth and quivering chin until his hand ached.

Gabe wandered off towards the rear of the house as Clay's thoughts swirled around him. *Why me God? Why would You bring me here? Don't you have someone else to pick on?*

"Sir! Come quickly!" Gabe's excited tone penetrated Clay's oppression, and he lifted his head.

"I found a well."

A kernel of hope sprang up in Clay, and he scrambled to his feet.

Mama's springhouse. Water!

"And lots of fresh tracks. A horse has been here, recently."

Jubilee is here. He's alive. The thought surged him forward, and he hobbled around the side of the house.

"Let's see what we've got." Clay grabbed the rusty handle on the wood door.

Inside the tiny shed stood a vine-covered stone wall. An ancient board covered the opening of the well. Clay slashed through the vines with his pocket-knife and found a metal bucket.

Useless. The bottom had rusted out leaving the sides dangerously ragged. Clay sawed the bucket from its rope. Gabe snagged a bucket and rope from their gear and Clay lowered the bucket, not far, maybe two feet, until the splash. He started hauling.

Water. Clean and clear.

He carried the water out to Selel, gasping as the frigid liquid sloshed onto his pants.

Selel nickered and smacked her lips, pushing closer.

Clay began to pour the water into a second bucket as the mare shoved her nose and guzzled greedily, ears flopping with each gulp.

Water sloshed out, splashing her face. She did not even blink. She drank another half bucket before heaving a contented sigh.

"This is a deep well," Gabe said as he hauled water for his horse and mule.

"Yup, my brother Eric and I dug it," Clay replied, leaning against the wall of the springhouse. "My father made us dig down 'til we hit the spring. Took us weeks. The walls caved twice. Almost buried us alive."

Clay shook his head. "I was ten years old. What kind of father makes a ten-year kid do that?" He dipped a cup into the bucket and took a sip.

Cold. Crisp.

"Your father saved us by making you dig this." Gabe took a deep drink from his cup.

"My father never saved anything."

But he could not deny that the water tasted incredible.

"These are grape vines," Gabe said, caressing one of the broad leaves growing up the side of the springhouse.

"Yeah. My father made his own wine. He wanted the grapes close to the well so he wouldn't have to water them."

"They're close all right. Just about in." Gabe smiled and examined a decimated bunch of fruit. "Looks like someone's been eating them, and the leaves. Your dad might have kept Jubilee alive too, with these grapes."

Gabe plucked one of the remaining fruits and held it between thumb and forefinger. He inspected it closely, lifting it toward the sun.

"Look, Mr. Westin. You can see the seeds inside. You know, sir, it's not how many seeds are in the grape that's amazing. It's how many grapes are in each seed. That tiny word *in* can make all the difference to someone's life."

Clay shrugged. Gabe's words felt like sandpaper against his already shredded nerves. He just wanted to find Jubilee and get back home. Quick. He nodded toward the pack mule. "How many buckets did you bring?"

"Three. One to carry, two to feed."

"Let's find something for Jube to drink from."

"Yes, sir. No water, no life."

Gabe watered the mule while Clay approached the old barn looking for something big that would hold water. *Nothin'. We've got to get water to Jubilee.* Gabe's words rang in his ears "No water, no life."

He would have to go into the barn.

Don't look. Focus on the task. The more he tried not to look, the stronger it called. A vertical shadow caught his eye. He knew it was there.

Finally, he peeked through the slats of the old barn to see if it still stood. And it did.

The round pen.

The place where the unthinkable had happened. Clay could *see* his father's face. Bloody. Desecrated.

You did it.

Clay had longed for that day. Or so he thought. The day he would be free from his old man, his father. But when it happened, it was terrible. And Clay knew he would never really be free. His old man would haunt him, own him, until the day Clay died.

Sissy. Coward.

He would never be free.

• CHAPTER 8 •

The Need

Clay emerged from the barn batting at the sticky cobwebs trailing from his hat. "Water. We need to get somethin' big that will hold water," he mumbled.

"How about a bathtub, Sir?" Gabe asked, pointing into the house.

Through a section of crumbling wall, barely visible amidst the wild roses, stood an enamel bathtub.

"That was Mama's. It weighs a ton," Clay said. "I know because it took all three of us, my father, Eric and me."

"I'll help you," Gabe offered.

"You'll have to carry it yourself," Clay snapped. "I'll keep lookin' for something we can actually use."

The shed, the old tool shed, on the far side of the house. Clay rounded the corner. The cinderblock shed looked in much better condition than the house. It still had a shape to it. The door hung askew, and the one window was broken, but otherwise, it looked much the same.

"Bathtub. Stupid bathtub. The thing weighs two hundred pounds. We'd never get it out," Clay muttered, jerking the door wide. The hinge gave way, and the door fell, scraping his bad arm. He took a deep breath. *Hold it together.*

Spiders and lizards scrambled to escape, alerted to the invasion by the sudden change in daylight. Clay looked around the dark space.

"Nothin' dang it!" He threw an old spade in frustration. The shovel hit something in the dark corner. The sound made Clay's heart jump. It sounded like something substantial. Something that might hold water.

He got his hands on it. *Big, dusty, with a lid? What the heck is it?* As soon as his hands touched the leather handles on the side, he knew. *Eric's footlocker.* He dragged it to the center of the shed, into the sunlight. It was bulky but not heavy; the flimsy padlock quickly dispatched with the spade.

Clay's hands shook as he tried to get the lock from the latch. He tossed it once it was free and flung back the lid. Fine dust particles rose in a cloud. He sneezed, then breathed in carefully, checking to see if another sneeze would come.

Nope. He rubbed his nose on the collar of his tee-shirt. *Stupid allergies.*

The scent of cedar and old mothballs wafted up. Eric's uniform. The uniform he was supposed to be buried in. Except he never came home. He was buried in a mass grave somewhere in France with most of his division.

Clay moved the uniform aside and found photos, Dad grinning, arm around Eric in uniform. Mama looking sad with Eric's arm around her. And a stack of yellowed envelopes with letters. From Eric.

Clay gently pulled the letters from the trunk. They were in chronological order. He opened the last letter. It began with no salutation. Just the date. Clay began Eric's dirt-smeared, and hastily scrawled letter.

June 12, 1943

Fighting's getting worse. Been raining for days and we been hunkered down in the same stinking bunker for a week. Mud is past our ankles. Food's gone. Clean water gone. All I want is sleep, dry feet, and a burger with cheese.

Germans are closing in and we have nowhere to fall back.

Mom and Dad, I love you.

You too little brother.

An image filled Clay's mind. Eric, face down in mud, drowning in muck. Too weak to pull himself up. The earth absorbing him, claiming him.

His father's rage-filled eyes reflecting the truth.

It should have been you.

Josh. Eyes fixed. Face down in the mire.

He could not breathe. His lungs refused to expand. Pressure built in his chest, like a cold hand pressing, pressing, pressing down. He dropped the letters and lunged for the door. "I've got to get outta' here."

He leaned against the wall outside, hands on his knees, breathing like he had just outrun a bear. He thought he might vomit and kept his head down for several moments. He pulled in one last trembly gasp before heading back to the springhouse. *Keep it together.*

"Hi," Gabe smiled, drawing a bucket from the well and dumping it in the bathtub.

"How the ...? How did you get that tub out here?"

"I carried it some, dragged it some. It's not that heavy," Gabe shrugged.

Clay stuck his fingers under the curled edge and tried to lift. Nothing. Not even a budge.

Weak.

He had to get away from here. "I'll take Selel and look for Jube. You keep filling." Clay said, looking around for the mare.

She had not wandered far. As he approached, she turned and ambled toward him, meeting him halfway.

She was smart. Kept the reins on one side, so she didn't step on them.

He looped the reins over the horn and searched for something to use as a mounting block.

Selel followed him to the pecan fallen tree and stood like a boulder as he hauled his body into the saddle.

Not pretty but he did it himself.

Now to find the colt. *What if we're too late? What if I can't find him? What if he doesn't remember me?* Clay gave Selel her head figuring she could find Jubilee just as easily as he. The mare headed down the east trail, ears forward.

Clay didn't see Jubilee, but he was pretty sure he heard him. He found plenty of hoof prints and a small pile of manure that looked less than 24 hours old. The poop was dark and hard, signs of a dehydrated empty horse.

He and Selel crashed around in the mesquite for a while more before turning back. He'd need Gabe's help to run the colt down.

Gabe had finished filling the tub when Clay returned.

"Let's go – I know about where he is. Heard him."

"Let's allow the need to draw him," Gabe suggested.

"What do you mean?"

"Jubilee needs you. Whether he knows it or not right now, he needs you. Let the need do what it was designed to do." Gabe started toward the barn. "I'm going to settle in."

Clay thought a minute. Made sense. He shrugged and nodded. *Come on Jube, come and drink. Come, get life.*

Come, Beloved. Come, get Life.

Clay looked around. The voice sounded so clear he wondered if Gabe had spoken but - no. Gabe was unpacking pots and utensils for dinner.

"I'm losin' it," Clay muttered, grabbing his bag. He settled under a tree, near the other horses, Selel at his heels. He sat for a moment, listening to the rhythmic breath of Selel and the mule. He found himself breathing slower. Relaxing. Breathing.

"Mr. Westin."

Gabe's voice came from above.

"What!" Clay's body jerked awake. He'd fallen asleep next to the fire. Curled up like a kitten on the ground. Gabe offered him a hand, and he got himself upright.

He peered around the campsite, exhausted and addled. The sun was starting to disappear behind the barn, not a cloud to see. No rain tonight. Not even humid, just hot.

He ran his fingers over his hair before replacing his hat.

"I've made some dinner, sir. Are you hungry?"

Clay's empty stomach complained. "I am," he inhaled the fragrance, "for the first time in a long time. What did you cook?"

"Roasted rabbit with rice pudding for dessert." Gabe handed him a shallow tin bowl with a spoon.

Clay gazed at Gabe. The boy reminded him of someone; he couldn't think who. He picked up his rabbit drumstick. The skin was crunchy, salty, the meat, chewy and juicy. He stuffed another bite into his already full mouth, wiping the juice from his chin on his shirt.

"How long you been ridin' horses?" Clay asked, tasting the pudding. The raisins had plumped with milk, and the sweetened rice was soft but not sticky. He could feel each grain with his tongue. Every bite felt like rejuvenation. He closed his eyes and relished the pleasant warmth from within.

Gabe smiled his easy smile. "All my life."

"I figured. You've got that mare real light. She's a joy to ride. Makes me miss 'em. Makes me miss her." *Shadow.*

Tears sprang up, and Clay's mouth wouldn't work for chewing. His inability to control his emotions appalled him.

He put his bowl on the ground and tried to regain his composure. "I'm sorry. I wish I could stop cryin'. I'll be better once we're away from here."

Gabe looked at him – felt like *into* him - with a tenderness that made him gasp. "No need to sorry, sir. I'm here *for* you."

Embarrassed, Clay began rummaging through his pack bag, looking for nothing; needing to look like he was searching for something important. His fingers touched an object that made him stop. It felt like - a matchbox? *Too big.*

He dug a little, got his fingers around it and pulled it through his rolled up underwear and socks.

A small book lay in his hands. It was Clay's little Bible -- just the New Testament. Josh had given it to him for Father's Day two years prior. It had been in the bag, unnoticed. Clay opened it, flipping the pages. His thoughts flipped with the pages to the day two years before.

They'd gone camping for the weekend. Last camping trip they ever took. If he'd a known it was the last ... well, he woulda' done things different.

> *"Happy Father's Day, Dad. I hope you can read the tiny letters." Josh had grinned across the campfire. "Don't worry. I'll read it to you, if you need me."*

And there the Bible had lain. For two years. Josh's face came to his mind, as clear as a photo. His mischievous smile, his red hair. Josh was so Evelyn; it was impossible to remember the one without the other.

I need you now, Josh.

Crybaby.

Clay fell over. He didn't care that he spilled. Didn't care that he hit the side of his head. Didn't care.

Gabe lifted him gently and propped him into his side, his arm around Clay's frail shoulders. They sat for long minutes, Clay's face contorted as he worked to gain control of his runaway emotions. He tried to pull against Gabe's embrace but hadn't the strength.

"I'm sorry, Gabe. Please forgive me." Clay could not look him in the face.

Gabe blinked softly. "Forgive you? For what?"

"For weepin', like a baby." He glanced up and was captured by the compassion in Gabe's eyes; so pure that Clay could only breathe it in.

"Sir, there is nothing wrong with crying. It is a good thing to do sometimes. You know Jesus wept when He heard Lazarus had died."

"Sometimes, I hear a voice," Clay glanced at Gabe. It seemed OK to continue. "These thoughts. Clear as day, in my head. They go around and round. Makes me want to die." Clay cringed inwardly. Gabe would probably think he was crazy. And why not? Prob'ly he was crazy.

"That is the desire of the enemy. To torture and destroy." Gabe agreed.

"The enemy? Like Satan?" Clay scoffed. "Why would he bother with me? I'm not worth messing with. I'm old, I'm tired, and anything that *was* good about me is dead."

"Why do you say that?"

"Because it's true. Evelyn and Josh. They were my life. I wake up every morning and wish I hadn't. Eli says I loved 'em too much. Do you think that's possible? To love someone too much?"

"No sir, I don't." Gabe shook his head. "Tell me about them. I've made some strong coffee. We can sit here awhile and talk."

Clay considered the young man for a moment. He was tired. Tired of holding on, tired of pretending, tired of trying.

He raised his hands. "I don't even know where to start."

"Just start with the first thing you think of."

Tell him. Tell him everything.

Part Two

• CHAPTER 9 •

Lion

Spring 1934

Clay closed the gate and headed toward the lake in the far back pasture, bamboo fish pole in one hand, shovel in the other. He'd won the fish pole off Eli in a bet.

Where Eli had gotten it, Clay didn't know or ask. Eli had a reputation for liftin' things.

He couldn't wait to try his hand at catching catfish or whatever else would nibble his bait. His mouth filled with saliva at the thought of fish fried in salty cornmeal, and maybe some taters.

The breeze picked up, and Shadow rushed past him swinging her head from side to side, inviting him to play. Most of her dark winter coat had shed out, and at a year, she'd transformed to a steel gray with dark dapples on her hindquarters.

She had her mama's build. Sturdy through the chest, with a great big engine in the back. Her face was refined, almost Arabian looking. She was the most beautiful filly Clay had ever seen.

A giant oak tree, roots dipping in the water, offered shade from the already intense sun. Clay rested the pole against the tree and began to dig for worms.

His father's small herd of broodmares strolled over, following their curious offspring. He stopped digging and watched as Shadow sniffed noses with the lead mare, popping her lips to signify fearful submission.

Clay grinned and stomped the shovel. She never popped her lips at him anymore.

The mares dispersed and searched for young grass while the foals and Shadow frolicked.

Clay grimaced as he impaled one of his worms and dropped the line in the water. He always felt bad for the worms and wondered if they understood their doom.

He felt a strong tug on the line almost immediately and pulled in a good-sized catfish. Clay dragged it up onto the shore so it couldn't flop back. He hated sticking his fingers down a cat's throat.

This one had hooked through the lip. He feathered a rope through the mouth and gills of the fish and threw it into the water. A couple more like that and he'd go to bed with a full belly. A lot easier to sleep when your belly is full.

He glanced back at Shadow and smiled. She had pancaked herself flat in the sun and looked dead asleep.

Clay caught five more fish, making for an impressive string. He had a couple more worms and stood in the shade of the oak debating whether to try for one more fish or release the captives.

A crow called out a raucous warning from a stand of scrub brush behind Clay. As he turned, a group of turkeys exploded, gobbling in alarm, straight up from the brush.

The mares snorted, raised their tails, and took their foals quickly to the far end of the pasture.

Clay shaded his eyes and strained to see what had caused such commotion.

Something moved just below the seed heads of the long grass. He couldn't make out what it was. Whatever it was it moved like a predator. Stealthy.

A coyote?

Now he couldn't see anything.

The saw-grass rustled and two black tipped ears popped into view. Then the head. A mountain lion, wide-mouthed and panting, disappeared into the blond grass.

Clay crumbled against the tree. Kept his eyes glued on the spot.

Where was it?

He flicked a glance up the tree. A branch. Within reach. He could climb. He could get himself over the water.

Could lions swim? He didn't know.

Where was it?

Ears and two round, golden eyes peeked up over the grass. Clay started to turn towards the tree. He moved slow, hoping it would not notice his intent.

But it did.

It left the grass cover and began to slink toward him; its hypnotic eyes locked onto his.

Move.

He couldn't.

The lion was now less than 30 feet from him. Her red spoon shaped tongue pulsated from between long teeth.

Clay could not take his eyes away.

The big cat flattened her ears. Bared her teeth. Gathered her hind legs for the attack.

Move.

He couldn't.

To his right, not 12 feet away, Shadow woke, raised her head, and blinked at Clay with sleepy eyes.

Shadow! He'd forgotten about Shadow.

The filly's movement diverted the cougar from Clay, and it launched straight at the young horse.

A fountain of ferocity exploded through Clay's paralysis. Teeth bared, he grabbed the pole. He charged the lion; leaped in front of his filly and planted his feet.

"You get away from her!" he screamed, swinging at the lion's face like a possessed thing.

The sharp edge of the bamboo sliced the cat's pink nostril drawing three large drops of blood. The mountain lion screamed and recoiled, momentarily lifting its ears in shock.

It flattened its ears again and snarled, showing long, yellow teeth. Clay growled back and readied himself, holding the pole over his shoulder like a baseball bat.

The big cat suddenly shrank down, its eyes drawn up and over Clay's left shoulder.

It whirled quickly and skulked away towards the thicket. Clay stood ready to defend Shadow, but the lion continued its retreat and disappeared into the bushes.

Clay's shoulders sagged in relief. He leaned on the pole for a moment, just breathing.

He heard a hoof stomp. Felt warm air on his neck.

Shadow and the broodmares had huddled up, shoulder to shoulder, directly behind him.

For protection.

But they looked like a formidable foe. And they had scared the lion off.

Clay's knees buckled; he fell back against Shadow, hysteria bubbling up, overtaking him. He collapsed onto his back and allowed himself the release of laughter. Tears welled and fell as he hooted, stomping the ground.

He desperately needed a breath.

The thought of dying from laughter hit him, which made him laugh even harder.

The horses gathered around him, snuffling his face, curious.

He breathed in.

Horse whiskers and blue sky filled his eyes. He got another breath. Got control.

Clay sat up and scanned the landscape for any sign of the lion, and still giggling grabbed the pole for support.

He lurched to his feet, fetched his string of fish, and headed home, his arm over Shadow's neck, mares, and foals pressing in all around him.

Couldn't wait to tell Eric.

But when he did, Eric told their father.

And Clay was sent to bed without dinner and with a belt to the butt for lyin'.

• CHAPTER 10 •

Christmas
December 25, 1935

Clay pulled the flimsy blanket up to his chin watching the first streaks of daylight through the window. A piece of straw from the makeshift mattress poked his back, and he shifted his weight.

Eric breathed rhythmically from his pile of blankets.

Clay hoped his father was right. That Santy Claus did not exist. Because if Santy Claus was real, well, Clay never got nothin'. They never even had a tree.

But Eli and everyone at school talked about nothing else. Some girl at school said her family didn't even put up their tree 'til Christmas Eve.

Maybe Mama had stayed up late.

Maybe.

Mrs. Martin had made the whole class write a paragraph about what they wanted for Christmas. It was kind of fun, imaginin'.

He'd made a list. A new halter for Shadow, a pretty one with a silver nameplate, some new boots, just his. Not holey hand-me-downs from Eric, and maybe a saddle. No, he had crossed the saddle off. Didn't want to make Santy mad.

And now it was Christmas morning. He could hear Mama clankin' in the kitchen.

He crept downstairs slowly, just in case. Each step brought him closer to possible treasure. His stomach went tight. He peered around the corner into the living room hopin'. Hopin'. Nothin'.

Clay shrugged his sagging shoulders. Santy Claus wouldn't come here even if he was real.

"Come and eat, while it's hot," Mama yelled from the kitchen. She placed the big pot on the table using her stained apron to protect her hands. "Clay, get the bowls."

His father strode in through the back door and Eric wandered down the stairs. Mama laid spoons down at each place and sat opposite Clay's father at the head of the table. She winked at Clay and smiled. Mama had a beautiful smile.

Clay sat on the broken three-legged stool. He had to keep his back straight against the kitchen wall and one foot planted on the floor, or it would toss him to the ground. He could pitch back and forth and make the two remaining legs squeak pleasantly. If he added a side-to-side motion, it felt sort of like riding a very wide horse.

He filled his spoon with oatmeal and maneuvered the sticky load into his mouth, rocking the sides of the spoon against the corners of his mouth to increase his capacity. The cereal needed salt, but they didn't have any. He imagined oatmeal with white sugar and butter.

At least the mush warmed his belly. He'd hoped for a fried egg, but the hens weren't laying. Too cold. He couldn't blame them. But he checked every morning anyway.

Soon, he thought. *And maybe we'll get a cow for milk and cream...*

"For God's sake, Clay, stop that infernal noise!" his father bellowed. Milton leaned across the table and cuffed Clay across the face with his open hand.

Clay's head reeled back with the impact. Oatmeal spewed from his mouth. His head bounced against the wall and knocked the stool out from under him. His backside impacted the dirt floor, and he bit through his tongue.

Warm blood filled his mouth. He gagged, then to his horror, heaved oatmeal all over the floor.

"Milton!" Mama shrieked.

But his father was already on his feet and gone.

Mama fell to her knees under the table. "Clay, honey, are you all right?" She rubbed his back and pulled gently on his shirt, drawing him out.

"What did I do?" Clay cried. "I didn't do nothin'."

He held his hand to his cheek as the sting subsided. One of his upper molars hurt. He reached his fingers in to check it. Loose. Maybe it would be okay if he left it alone.

All he wanted to do was ride away. Take Shadow and never come back.

The vomit lay in a steamy pile. He couldn't look at it, or there would be more. He rose slowly, knees shaking.

He wanted to kick the stupid stool but was sure he'd land on his butt again.

Mama put her arms around his thin shoulders and led him to the sink. She pumped clean cold water into a bucket, dipped the corner of her apron in and began wiping the vomit and blood from his mouth. "Here," she handed him a glass of water, "rinse."

Clay swished the water around and spat pink. "Why does he hate me?"

"He doesn't hate you, Clay. He's your father."

"Then why is he so mean?" Clay stared into her blue eyes and found only sadness.

"I don't know, son. I don't know." She began cleaning up the pile as Clay cleared the remaining dishes.

Eric, unfazed at the end of the table, scraped his bowl with a spoon and tossed the dish in the pan.

His father stood in the living room, warming his big hands over dying embers. He poked at a chunk of wood from the outer part of the fireplace, encouraging the flame to flare. His black hair flopped into his dark eyes, and he seemed lost in thought.

"It's Christmas, Milton. Can we go to church?" Mama asked, her voice straining with artificial brightness.

"What for?" he asked with a snarl, turning around to warm his backside

"Please, Milton. For me." Mama begged. "It can be my Christmas gift."

His frown deepened. "Why do you get a Christmas gift when nobody else does?"

"Clay," Mama called. "Clay, honey, do you want to go to church? It's Christmas. Everyone goes to church on Christmas." She knelt in front of him, her eyes locked on his.

He didn't want to. But his mother's eyes were desperate. "Yeah," he replied. *This is my Christmas gift to you*. "I want to go."

"Thank you," she mouthed, eyes brimming.

"Eric," Dad said, "do you want to go to church?"

Eric, 15 years old, and dark like his father, dropped his load of wood on the hearth. "I don't care," he looked up. "Will they have food?"

Mama clapped her hands. "They might. Please, Milton. The boys want to go."

Clay watched his father roll his eyes and exhale and knew that his mother had gotten her wish. They put on the best clothes they had and slicked their hair with water. Clay's hair was oily enough he didn't need any pomade, not that they had any.

Mama put on her good dress and pinched some color into her pale cheeks. The sparkle in her eyes was real, and Clay had never seen her so lovely.

They climbed into the beat up Model A and headed into Nede.

"We're gonna' be late," Clay's father said. "Church started at 9:00."

"I don't mind," Mama replied, pulling on a pair of white gloves.

"I do," he growled. "We ain't stayin' if I gotta' walk in late."

The Westin family marched up the slate lined walkway to the entrance of the old brick church at 9:15.

They were early. The Christmas service began at 9:30, to allow for the Christmas only crowd.

A tall, well-dressed man greeted them as they walked in the front doors. He was taller than Clay's father - maybe six feet and then some, and he wore the shiniest boots Clay had ever seen. A prosperous belly hung over his silver belt buckle.

"Merry Christmas, folks. I'm Sam Mayfield." His booming voice sounded warm, and his blue eyes crinkled at the corners.

Clay had a passing thought of Santy Claus.

Next to Mr. Mayfield, passing out leaflets, stood a young girl. Her wide-set eyes were only a couple shades lighter than her emerald green dress. Two thick auburn braids adorned her shoulders.

She offered a leaflet to Clay's father, who raised his hand imperiously to decline.

"This is Evelyn, my daughter. Welcome to First Baptist." Mr. Mayfield reached to shake Milton's hand.

"What's yer name?" Milton cocked his head but hid his hand behind him.

"Sam. Sam Mayfield. Just moved here from North Carolina. I bought the Crawford place. Been a lawyer for 30 years. Now I'm going to try my hand at ranching."

"Crawford's place?" Milton's dark eyes glittered; red traveled up into his face.

"Yes!" Mr. Mayfield looked thrilled. "You know it?"

"Backs up to my place. Been settin' there a year." Milton's words slipped from between clenched teeth.

Mr. Mayfield didn't seem to notice. "Yes. The house needs some work. But the price. I couldn't say no." Sam retracted his arm, but his smile did not change. He gazed directly into Milton's face. "I'm delighted to meet some neighbors."

Clay's father stiffened and walked away. "Guess so."

Mama shook Mr. Mayfield's hand warmly enough to make up for her husband.

Evelyn smiled straight into Clay, her green eyes sparkling. His stomach tumbled, but he could not look away. She offered him a leaflet, extending it with long, graceful fingers.

Clay took the paper, not certain what it was for. He glanced at the front, opened it. Too many words. Looked back at her. She still smiled.

Smile back, stupid. He managed a lop-sided grimace and closed the leaflet.

When he looked up, his family was far ahead, entering the sanctuary.

He took a few hasty strides, but he could feel her eyes on him. He peeked over his shoulder.

She was still smiling at him. Clay smiled back at her and collided with Eric's back.

"What's wrong with you?" Eric hissed.

"Nuthin," Clay retorted.

The usher directed the Westins to a mostly empty row in the front. The church smelled like pine from the evergreen boughs in each of the windows. Clay's father filed in first, followed by Eric, and then Mama, who sat between Eric and Clay to prevent any foolishness.

They had not sat long before the show began. The preacher entered through a door behind the altar. "Merry Christmas!"

he hollered, opening his hymnal. "Let us stand and sing, 'Joy to the World!'"

Clay had no singing voice. At least he knew he couldn't sing and didn't try. The old woman behind him couldn't sing either, but what she lacked in pitch she tried to make up for in volume. She leaned forward over the pew, so close Clay could smell her old stinky breath. She squeezed her eyes tight in religious ecstasy while bawling the hymn as loudly as she could.

Clay turned and stared in disbelief. His mother shot him a warning glance, so he dropped his eyes and shuffled sideways out of range.

He surveyed the stained glass windows. One window on the southern side of the church showed a man hanging on a cross, blood pouring from His side.

Clay hated to think about blood. Ever since he witnessed Midnight's life flowing from her, he'd been queasy about the whole subject.

Mercifully, the singing ended, and they sat on the hard wooden pews.

"And now," the preacher announced, "Evelyn Mayfield will come to read from the Book of Mark."

She made her way down the aisle and stood in front of the congregation, but her green eyes remained on Clay.

"And there were shepherds watching their flocks by night. And an angel of the Lord ..."

He was mesmerized.

She finished reading. The preacher bounded from his chair and placed his arm around Evelyn.

"Let us pray!" the preacher bellowed, waving his arm expansively. Almost everyone bowed their heads, except Clay and Evelyn. She gazed at the window with the picture of the bleeding man. There was a look on her face. It could only be called adoration.

Clay felt the inside of his throat grow hot and tight. He couldn't cry, not here. In front of his father and everyone. Evelyn's expression filled him with a hunger he could not make sense of. She was different from anyone else he had ever met.

The preacher took his place in the pulpit and began the sermon. He told them about Jesus, the Godman, coming to earth long ago and being born in a manger, and dying on the cross for sin.

Clay understood sin. Didn't his father call him a dirty little sinner?

The preacher concluded his sermon with a flourish, inviting one and all to come forward and escape the torment of Hell. Mr. Mayfield and the other ushers walked down the aisle, escorting anyone who so desired, to come forward and be saved.

Clay knew he needed saving. He needed saving from all sorts of things. And he knew about Hell. Clay's mother took his hand and pulled him upright as Mr. Mayfield approached their row. Clay's gaze slipped sideways meeting his father's. He was surprised by the hurt he saw.

Clay continued down the aisle anyway, propelled by strong need and his mother's iron grasp. He knelt and folded his hands like his mother did. Mr. Mayfield stood over them.

"Would you like to receive Jesus as your savior?"

Clay looked up into Mr. Mayfield's face. "Yes, sir. I want saving."

"Do you understand that you have sinned and offended God's holy law?"

"Yes, I understand," Clay hung his head in shame. *Many times, I have offended.*

"Do you trust on Jesus Christ to pay for your sins?"

Clay's eyes filled as he thought of it. "Yes, I trust Jesus." He had to wipe his nose with his sleeve, but Mama didn't seem to notice.

"God loves you, son, and He has a wonderful plan for your life if you will obey Him."

Clay's head snapped up. "Really?" he said earnestly. "All I have to do is obey?"

Mr. Mayfield smiled and placed his big hand on Clay's head. His touch was warm and gentle. "Yes, son. Just trust and obey."

Clay knew he and Mama were in trouble the moment his fanny hit the pew. His father's face first flushed red, then turned white with anger. The mound of muscles in his jaw clenched and unclenched as the service concluded.

Clay bowed his head and studied his tired looking shoes.

He could not look around for Evelyn or Mr. Mayfield. He felt bad about that. He would have liked to say good-bye.

They trailed single file to the car. His father waited until everyone was trapped before letting it fly. "Do you know who that was? That Sam Mayfield? He bought the Crawford Ranch. I was gonna' buy that ranch." His face throbbed with red rage. He slammed his open hand into the steering wheel. "This is your fault, Pearl. If you had gotten the money from your parents..." He thought another moment. "An you left me and Eric sittin' there lookin' like idiots! You are never goin' back. Do you understand?"

Mama's back went stiff and stared at her hands the whole way home until the car turned down the long dirt driveway. Then she moved her stare out the window, her face a tightly controlled mask of calm.

The car stopped.

Clay's father turned and placed his arm over the seat. His dark eyes glinted sharp. "I want you boys to change clothes and clean the stalls," Clay heard the edge in his voice, and he knew that cold, dead look.

He tried to catch Mama's eye but she concentrated on her gloved hands, her breath came quickly, in small, panicked inhalations. Her lips moved silently, and Clay wondered if she was praying to their new God.

"Do you hate him?" Clay asked Eric, his hands aching from his death-grip on the pitchfork. He kept his ears open but heard nothing. She wouldn't cry out. Clay imagined driving the sharp, dirty tines into his father. For Mama. For himself.

"Nah," Eric replied hawking up a ball of phlegm and spitting it outside the door. "I stay outta' the way and do as I'm told."

"I try to do as I'm told," Clay shook his head. "I don't know what he wants half the time."

"Jus' stay out of his way and you'll be alright."

But Clay could not seem to stay out of his father's way no matter how he tried.

• CHAPTER 11 •

Auction
March 1936

Clay loved the spring livestock auction. He and Eric had rounded up 20 two-year-old steers for the sale and herded them through town toward the feedlots. The air had lost its morning coolness and sweat beaded on Clay's nose. He adjusted his hat for maximum shade.

The boys drove the steers past the pavilion where the ranchers ate sandwiches and drank lemonade.

The fragrance of sizzling beef made his tongue dance. If they got a good price, maybe he and Eric could split a patty melt.

Evelyn Mayfield sat on a bench eating an ice-pop while her father inspected a group of heifers. Her eyes grew wide as Clay rode by on Shadow. Made Clay even warmer.

The boys drove their cattle into a lot, closed the gate and began the long wait for the auction. Their father wouldn't arrive until the afternoon. He fancied himself a livestock man, but rarely had money to buy. Milton preferred whiskey when he had the cash.

Clay and Eric wandered to an open arena and watched as some of the cowboys timed each other cutting cattle from the herd. Eric reached out and popped Clay's shoulder. "You try it."

Clay scoffed, "I don't even have a saddle."

"Try it. I'll give you a quarter."

"Where'd you get a quarter?"

"Hey!" Eric called. "Over here, my little brother wants a try."

One of Mr. Mayfield's hands rode over. "You want my pony? You can't ride your mare; you don't even have a bridle."

"Nope," Clay answered. "I'll ride Shadow."

Mr. Mayfield's man opened the gate for him, smirking as Clay rode past into the arena. He guided Shadow through the herd, dividing the group. He pointed at the cow he'd chosen. A red roan with half a tail, and some wicked long horns. The gate-keeper nodded.

Clay sat and squeezed.

Shadow rocked back on her hindquarters and launched from a stop to a dead run in one step. Clay focused on the cow, squinting so hard his ears hurt.

Shadow's ears pinned flat against her head as she stayed on the cow. They moved like one unit as Shadow first cut the cow from the herd, then dodged back and forth, to keep it theirs.

One hard push to the left nearly separated them, but Shadow managed to slide herself back under him. They kept the roan cow separate from the herd and drove it around the opposite side of the arena.

Clay tipped his hat to the cow and relaxed his gaze. Shadow stopped so fast she raised a dust cloud. The cow galloped past them to the safety of her herd.

Clay turned back to where Eric stood. He couldn't see him because a large crowd had gathered in the very spot Eric had been. Clay, confused, scratched his head and looked about.

Mr. Mayfield approached at a jog, shaking his head. "How did you do that?"

"I dunno," Clay shrugged. "I do it every day at home."

"I've never seen anything like it. Is that mare for sale?"

"No! No sir."

"I figured." Mr. Mayfield patted Shadow's sweaty neck. "You ever decide to sell her I'll pay whatever you need to get." Sam extended his hand to Clay. "Deal?"

"Yessir," Clay agreed, shaking his hand like a grown-up. "If I ever need to sell her, I'll let you know."

Evelyn waved to him from her perch on the top rail of the fence. A thrill shot through him, and he waved back, grinning like an ape. The crowd dispersed, and Eric's dark head came back into view.

"What was that about?" Clay said, sliding off Shadow.

Eric shook his head. "I don't know, mebbe' they've never seed a kid ride like you. I know I haven't."

Clay dropped the lead rope so Shadow could search for sparse tufts of grass.

"Aren't you afraid she'll wander off?"

"No," Clay furrowed his brow, surprised by the question. "Why would she leave me?"

"No reason," Eric rolled his eyes and shook his head. "Look. There's that red headed gal you're so sweet on."

Clay's head jerked up, "where?"

"Gotcha'," Eric guffawed. "I knew you were sweet on her."

Clay watched Evelyn as she headed back toward the pavilion. She turned in Clay's direction and their eyes locked.

He heard nothing, saw nothing, except those big green eyes.

A bellow from Eric broke his gaze. "Bull loose!"

Clay quickly focused on the monstrous red Longhorn bull. It had broken through its pen and was trotting straight for its cows, huge dewlap flapping with each stride.

Evelyn stood directly in its path, her face frozen in terror.

Clay looked wildly for Mr. Mayfield. No sign of him.

Clay lunged for Shadow, pushing his fingers into her chest. She dropped to her knees, and he grabbed a chunk of mane and swung himself up. He squeezed and focused, and they went for the bull at a dead run.

Get between 'em, then figger it out.

The bull shied to the left and shook his horns, threatening a cowboy who waved his hat in a vain attempt to distract the animal. Clay and Shadow dodged between the feedlots, galloping around them.

Faster. We gotta' go faster.

Shadow burst through the feedlot maze and pivoted to face the bull. Her ears were flat against her head as she snaked her head in challenge.

"Hey!" Clay screamed at the bull. "Get away!"

The massive animal stopped, confused by Shadow's aggressive movements. It stepped to the right and attempted to charge through. Clay grabbed a handful of mane and clung on as the mare and bull began a dangerous dance of back and forth, left and right.

Three hard maneuvers to the left and a cowboy got a lasso over the bull's horns. Two more men threw their ropes, and the bull was had.

Shadow snorted and dropped her head, sides heaving from the effort.

Clay felt the blood drain from him. His belly went weak; his heart hammered in his chest. He felt like.... dang... he was gonna'. He leaned over Shadow's neck and puked.

Clay wiped his mouth with shirt sleeve and looked for Evelyn. She was in her daddy's arms. Safe.

Sam Mayfield caught Clay's eye and nodded his thanks.

• CHAPTER 12 •

Love

Clay peeked into Mrs. Parker's seventh grade class from the doorway. Evelyn sat in the first row which made staring at her more difficult. He had a strategy worked out. He had to be quick about it. Didn't want Eli to catch wind. He'd never hear the end.

If she glanced up, he would pretend he was looking out the window, or he could shift his attention completely away to the American flag in the corner of the room. A patriotic moment.

She did look up. Clay could not move. Evie smiled. Not a secret smile but a delighted-didn't-care-who-saw-her smile. Clay stepped into the doorway and grinned.

Eli slapped him on the back.

"Whatcha' staring at?" Eli whispered. Then he saw. "Aw, c'mon. Yer gonna' get in trouble. And I'm hongry."

He spied her later that day, after classes, all hunkered down over something in the front yard of the school. He approached quietly. As Clay came even closer, he could see in her hands, a nest with four tiny birds.

They were hatchlings, featherless and shriveled. Three were so weak they could not hold up their own heads. The fourth though, stretched upwards on his little legs, blindly gaping, proclaiming his need to anyone who would notice.

"What are they?" Clay asked, drawing back involuntarily.

"They're Mockingbirds," she sniffled. "Their nest must have blown out of a tree."

"Whatcha' gonna' to do with 'em?"

"Feed them, if I can. They need worms." Evelyn stopped crying for a moment as she considered Clay. "Would you help me? Could you find worms and chop them up?"

Clay gulped. *Chopping worms*. He couldn't think of anything he'd rather not do. He'd be late getting home. He would likely get a whippin'.

But he gazed into Evelyn's face. Her splotchy cheeks, her unashamed tears, her long, stuck-together eyelashes appeared even longer. She looked like a heartbroken angel.

Clay glanced over at Shadow. The mare grazed quietly on the long line.

"Yeah. I'll help you," he replied.

Her watery smile more than made up for the fishy smell the worms left on his hands when he chopped them up.

"You have to push the food all the way past the tongue, or they'll suffocate," she explained, pulling a dull pencil from her bag.

Clay watched, entranced, as she gently filled the tiny mouths, avoiding the hole under the tongue that would have killed them. The tip of Evie's own tongue poked through her pursed lips as she concentrated.

"I raised Shadow," he offered.

Evie looked up from her maternal duty. "How come?"

"Her mama died. Bled to death right after Shadow came."

"She thinks you are her mama,"

"Yeah," he grinned. "That she does."

He continued watching her long fingers carefully balance worms atop the pencil and guide the glop into the waiting mouths.

Their foreheads brushed, and Evie gazed up into Clay's eyes. Something inside of him broke free, and it seemed he'd known her forever.

Evie's cheek dimpled, and she shifted her attention back to the hatchlings. "I think I'll call this one Seymour," she said, holding the little bird with the big mouth.

"Whatcha' got there sweetheart?" Mr. Mayfield stood over them, peering down.

Clay jumped at the sound of Mr. Mayfield's voice. He felt mortified, as though he'd been caught doing something sinful.

"Mockingbirds, Daddy. Clay chopped worms for them."

Mr. Mayfield smiled at Clay. "She is forever rescuing something. Just like her mother. Thank you, son, for helping her. It's good to see you again."

Sam Mayfield escorted Evie to his car while Clay called Shadow. Evie cradled her tiny orphans in one hand and waved to Clay from the back seat of the Buick. He returned the wave, threw his leg over Shadow, and trotted the whole way home, singing "You Are My Sunshine."

• CHAPTER 13 •

Dancer

June 1939

"Clay Westin!" Evelyn's voice carried down the school hallway.

He'd not gotten far cleaning out his locker. Only had a couple days before school let out for summer. Maybe forever. Clay wasn't sure he'd go on to 9th grade.

He slammed the door and spun around, hoping she had not seen his mess.

Evelyn sashayed toward him, her skirt swishing around her ankles. She wore her red hair down her back in a ponytail with a blue ribbon.

Even the air around her smelled good. She pushed a stray lock of hair behind her ear and smiled. *Her eyes.*

"Yeah?" he tried to sound casual, but his voice broke, and he swallowed the end of the word.

"Sign my yearbook?"

"Uh. Okay." Why couldn't he ever talk around her?

"Here, use my back." She whirled around.

He propped the book against her warm shoulders. *Her hair.* Her hair smelled like roses. What should he say? He couldn't think of anything. Not true. He wanted to write *I love you* but that would be stupid.

"Are you coming tomorrow night?" she demanded, half turning and dislodging the book.

Clay felt confused and unsure where to place the yearbook. "What's tomorrow night?"

"School talent show," she huffed. "I'm dancing."

He must have looked surprised.

"Ballet," she elaborated, opening her eyes wide, like he should know.

"I, I guess so," he shrugged. "What time?" How would he get there? He would walk. He would walk on his hands if he had to.

"Starts at 7:00."

She turned around so he could write.

He scrawled his name on the front cover of her book and handed it back. She stared at him, expectantly.

"Uh." *Dang it.* He shrugged apologetically. "I don't have a yearbook."

"Oh," she said softly, hugging her book to her chest. "I'm sorry, Clay." Her expression changed, and he knew she knew why.

"It's okay." He hadn't even thought about the yearbook. Until now.

"See you tomorrow." There was no hint of question. She pirouetted and started down the hall.

"Hey," he called out.

"Yes?" she spun around.

He loved the way one cheek dimpled when she smiled. "Whatever happened to them baby birds?"

"Three died, but my dad helped me with Seymour. He grew up and flew away," she fluttered her hands. "Thank you for helping me that day."

"Anytime," he replied, meaning it.

She continued down the hall. Clay remained for several seconds, just breathing her air.

Milton agreed they could go to the talent show.

"What talent do you have?" Eric teased as they washed up after supper.

"None," Clay admitted.

Eric stared at him, "Clay, you do things with horses I've never seen anyone else do. I guess you'd have a hard time getting a horse in the auditorium - plus, we'd need a big broom and basket in case he ... you know." Eric chortled, apparently tickled by the image of a horse pooping on stage.

The school auditorium was dark and whispery until a spotlight flashed onto Betty-Jo. She peered into the audience, blinking into the bright light. She cleared her throat loudly and nodded to the pianist. The music started, and Betty-Jo began to sing. Painful.

The next contestant, a boy in Eli's class who played the trumpet, made Betty-Jo sound good. Clay heard the boy's mother bragging, "that's my son," from three rows back. *I'd keep my mouth shut if he was mine,* Clay thought.

Milton squirmed in his chair and looked around impatiently, clearly wanting to leave. He glared at Clay with an accusing look.

Evelyn was last. The curtain parted, and the spotlight glared upon her.

She stood as still as death on one pointed toe, bent at the waist, slim arms open in front of her as if embracing the audience. She wore a yellow mid-length skirt, the color of butter; her red hair pulled back in a chignon.

Clay's mother inhaled and grasped his arm. "Is that Evelyn?" She whispered in his ear, "Oh, Clay, she's lovely."

He didn't know how to respond. Evelyn wasn't his, but his mother's comment made him feel possessive. Like she might be. A tiny flicker of hope burned deep inside Clay's soul.

The needle dropped onto the phonograph in a scratchy, sputtery sound, then her music began, and she started to dance.

She leaped, pirouetted and spun dizzyingly on one toe. Clay was hypnotized. He had never seen anyone move so joyously, so alive. So beautiful.

The music ended, and the spotlight died. The stage went dark.

Clay spontaneously jumped to his feet, clapping his hands so hard they stung. Others around him stood as well. *How could they not?*

As the auditorium lights flickered on, Clay's mouth required closing. He snuck a peek at Mama, she peeked back, and smiled, her eyes shimmery with tears.

Women wiped their eyes, some of the men blew their noses. No one seemed untouched. Except Milton. He groaned and tipped out of his chair. "Let's go," he hissed. "I don't want to get stuck in the parkin' lot."

In the car on the way home, Clay's father caught his eye in the rear view mirror. "She's not for the likes of you, you know. You ain't got nuthin' a girl like that would want."

Clay felt the blood drain from his face. He couldn't swallow. He covered his throat and saw the look in his father's eyes.

Satisfaction.

Mama stared out the window, shaking her head.

• CHAPTER 14 •

Broken

The little chestnut stallion pressed his body against the farthest edge of the round pen. Apart from a breeze ruffling his mane, the horse did not move.

Clay recognized the type of horse. Some horses expressed everything with their bodies. Others went inside themselves. This one would disappear inside himself if pushed. Clay rested, his body passive. These horses needed time. Time to think, process and respond. Clay waited for him to blink.

Only after the horse had released a huge breath and licked his lips did Clay pick up the end of the long rope.

Milton's work was evident on the horse's legs and head. Rope burns and swollen contusions from yesterday's lesson. Clay knew what it was like to be chased, beaten, shamed.

"I won't hurt you," he whispered.

Clay's fingers were gentle on the rope, slowly drawing the horse to him. The horse pulled back against the feel of the halter. Clay stayed steady, then slowly increased the feel on the rope. Not too much pressure, not too little.

Several seconds and the horse moved toward him. Clay opened his hands releasing all pressure. He waited until the horse blinked and licked his lips again.

Clay picked up the rope a second and third time. By the fourth time, the horse seemed curious. Clay casually took up the slack, his body quiet, relaxed. He averted his eyes, breathed slowly, conscious of the effect his body had on the horse.

The stallion pulled back as the rope created a visible connection between them. Clay stood steady again until the horse came forward to relieve the pressure on his poll. Again, immediate release.

Clay repeated this procedure until he could pretend to draw gently on the rope and the horse came.

"I'm not going to eat you," Clay rubbed the stallion's forehead. The little horse stepped closer.

"What are you doin' boy?"

Clay spun around, excited to show his father the progress they'd made.

"I'm gettin' him used to the rope, Dad. He'll tie better if he knows how to make the pressure go away."

His father's big hand struck Clay's face as quickly as a rattler. "Gimme' that, Clay. I swear you ain't worth the dirt God used to make you. I tole you to tie him. Like this."

Milton threw a loop around the chestnut's foreleg. "I'm gonna' show you how to break a stud colt quick. "Get outta' the way."

He snubbed the rope tight around the post in the center of the pen and whipped the horse's rump with the other end. The horse plunged forward and down, his neck arched between his front legs. He rolled on his side and lay, ribs heaving. Milton moved in and lassoed his other foreleg. He moved quickly, like a dancer, and had all four legs bound.

Milton threw another rope over the horse's head and tied it to the post. "Sit on his head."

Clay stared at his father. "Sit on his head?"

"I'm gonna' cut him. I need you to sit on his head."

"Cut him? Cut what?" He couldn't move.

Milton rolled his eyes, grabbed Clay's arm and pushed him down until he straddled the horse's face.

"I'm gonna' castrate him. Now you see he stays down. Hear?"

Clay could only nod. Between his knees, the horse's nostrils flared and Clay heard and felt the muscular tension as his father sliced. The horse tried twice to rise, but Clay's weight on his head kept him prone.

"I'm sorry. I'm sorry. I'm so sorry." Clay whispered, stroking the horse's cheek with his fingers. He clamped his eyes, but hot tears rolled, spilling onto the horse's muzzle.

"O.K. Clay. We're done."

Clay rose.

The blood. It covered his father's hands, the horse's back legs, it ran in streams into the dirt. The little horse lay still, eyes closed.

Clay's father loosened the ropes from the snubbing post, but the little horse did not move. He removed the ropes from the legs and still the horse did not stir. Finally, Milton poked the horse with his pointy-toed boot. Nothing.

"Let him lay. We'll come back tomorrow."

"I'll get him some water."

Clay's father glared. "Did you hear nuthin'? He'll have water when he rides good."

"But he's had no water all day!"

"It's just a horse, Clay. It's not like he has feelings or nuthin'. You know what?" Milton's head collapsed back as though Clay had drained him. "Just forget it." Milton stared at Clay like he had just realized something. "There's no way you're my kid. Go do somethin' useful like helpin' your ma in the kitchen."

Clay's heart pounded as he stole a glance at the horse and escaped out the gate.

"I'm not his." And Clay was glad.

Clay woke the next morning with a fever and searing throat. Mama hovered over him, covering his forehead with cool rags, making him sip catnip tea. It tasted vile. Even adding sugar didn't cut the bitterness. She made him drink every drop.

By the next day, Clay could not swallow his own spit. He began drifting in and out of consciousness. He knew he was wetting himself but couldn't care. He heard voices, saw his mother and Eric, but could not respond. His body had no strength.

He heard his mother crying, pleading. "Please, Milton. Please!" She sounded far away. He could not remember how he got to the car. He did remember Mama weeping and rocking and pleading. She had his head in her lap, her cool fingers smoothing his hair back from his face. Her tears mixed with his sweat, and she wiped them away with the rag. She held his face in her hands "Clay David. You stay with me; you hear? Promise me."

He could only blink, but she understood.

"Faster, Milton. Drive faster."

•

Clay woke on his back in a strange white bed, in a strange white place. He wondered vaguely if he was in Heaven.

He moved. A sharp pain in his chest made him gasp. Mama lifted her head from the chair next to his hospital bed. Their eyes met, and she leaned forward.

"Oh, you are back! You scared me so!"

He tried to move his lips, but they refused.

She brought ice chips and fed them to him, one by one, with a spoon.

He tried not to but could not keep back a soft moan.

"Are you hurting, son?"

He nodded and dropped his hand onto his chest.

"I'll get the doctor."

"He is lucky to be alive," he overheard the doctor just outside the curtain. "He has a significant heart murmur which may or may not improve. His right knee was also affected by the Rheumatic Fever. Only time will tell. He needs rest for several months. Bring him back to see me at my office in a month. And Mrs. Westin, you need to know. He will likely be sterile. Unable to have children."

•

For the first month, Clay slept and slept. By the second month, he could feel his energy returning. The morning his legs could carry him downstairs he ventured out after breakfast.

He ached to see Shadow, brush her, run his hands down her face.

He looked in the barn. She wasn't there. He checked the paddock. Not there either. He whistled. No reply. Maybe she'd been turned out with the broodmares in the back pasture. He caught his breath. The mountain lion. What if it got her while he was sick? Blood drained from his face, and he felt suddenly cold. His weakened heart floundered.

Clay staggered toward the house. He had to know. A noise caught his ear. Eric pulling weeds in the garden.

"Shadow?" Clay panted.

Eric straightened and stared for a moment. "They didn't tell you?"

He knew it. "No," he whispered.

"Clay," Eric dropped the weeds and held out his hands helplessly. "Clay, Dad sold Shadow. There was no money to pay the hospital ..."

Clay's knees buckled. He lay in the garden, too stunned to cry, too weak to scream. He could only writhe on the ground, inhaling dirt with each gasp. His fists opened and closed spasmodically, grabbing handfuls of grass.

"Ma!" Clay heard Eric yell. "Somethin's wrong with Clay."

Clay heard the back door slam and his mother begging as she ran, "Oh, God, please." She fell next to him, pulling him onto her legs. "Clay," she screamed, shaking him gently.

He looked at her and closed his eyes.

She wiped the dirt away from his mouth. "We had to, son. We had no choice. We had to." She crushed him to her chest, weeping.

I will never give my heart to anyone again, Clay vowed.

•

Clay sat on the front porch, and imagined a faceless cowboy whipping Shadow, misunderstanding her, scaring her. That was the worst. Seeing Shadow's fear.

Mama brought him a glass of water from the springhouse. It was ice cold, so cold that if you drank too fast, your teeth and head would throb.

"You will be all right," she sank down on the step next to him. Her body hunched over as she tried to look into his eyes.

"Who did he sell Shadow to?"

"I don't know, Clay. One of his friends, I guess."

"Mr. Mayfield wanted her. He would have paid a lot for her."

"We didn't know that, son. Your father was frightened for your life. We thought we were going to lose you."

"He tole me he wasn't my father," Clay whispered. He pushed his chin up into his quivering lips. "I hate him."

"Oh, Clay," her hand flew to her mouth. "Don't say that." She shook her head. "He is your father. He gave you life!"

"Then why would he say that?"

Mama sat up straight, smoothing her apron over her lap. She looked away for a moment, composing her thoughts.

Her shoulders softened, and she gazed into Clay's eyes. "Clay," she pressed her lips together. "Before you were born I left your father. I took Eric -- he was just a little boy - and left. My mother sent me money, and I took the train back home to

Virginia. I didn't want to be with your father anymore. You know why I think."

Clay nodded. *Yes.*

"My mother had worried about me. She was happy to have me back. Thrilled to see Eric."

Mama's chin shook. "My dad though - he wasn't happy. I don't think he ever forgave me for running off with your father. See, my dad warned me." She looked away and seemed to shrink down a little.

"He warned me that your dad was just after money. I didn't believe him. Your father was so handsome and strong - a railroad worker. He just... just swept me away. He'd ramble on about Texas. It all sounded so romantic. He wanted to buy a ranch, raise cattle. I thought... Well, let's say I thought it would be different. Life would be different.

"I hadn't been home long, a couple weeks. I discovered I was pregnant. With you."

She breathed out with a heaviness that ripped the seam around Clay's soul. He could not move or breathe. He was undone. He fixed his eyes on the dirt.

You. If not for you, she would be free. Safe.

"My father sent me back, here," Mama continued. "He said I'd made my bed; now I could sleep in it. I think your father suspected I'd gone somewhere else but I didn't. I just went home. I just wanted to go home..." Her voice trailed off. She seemed consumed by her own thoughts.

She turned suddenly and gripped his shoulders with strong fingers. "Clay." Mama's eyes blazed fervent. "You are not a bastard. You are Milton Westin's son. No matter what he says. You hear me?"

Clay nodded but had trouble keeping his head straight. It seemed too heavy for his neck.

Mama went on. "Your father sold Shadow because we needed the money. There wasn't another horse on this ranch that could have paid your bill." Tears gathered in her blue eyes, but she continued. "Shadow loved you. She would be glad to know she saved you."

Mama's tears dropped unheeded. She drew him into her side. "That's what love does, Clay. It gives when there is nothing left to give. You are lucky to have had Shadow. Most folks never get to love anything that much."

Clay dropped into her lap. He wept, great heaving sobs. Pouring out his pain. Her pain. Pearl rocked him and rubbed his back.

They did not hear his father's footsteps. Clay only heard his ugly voice from overhead when it was too late to pretend.

"What the ... What are you doin' out here? Cryin' like an infant," his father spoke with outraged intensity. "You think you got problems boy? Try bein' a man. Real men don't cry."

Clay crept up to a sit. He kept his eyes on the rough wood of the porch. *Don't say nuthin' Just hold it together.*

His father stormed off leaving Clay and Mama on the porch with their shame.

Mama rubbed her face, pressing her fingertips against her eyes. She rose stiffly and walked back to the kitchen.

Real men don't cry.

He never cried over Shadow again.

• CHAPTER 15 •

Back at the Ranch

Clay looked at Gabe, then around the old homestead. The sky had darkened, but his soul felt lighter. "Any sign of Jube?"

"No, but he'll be along."

Clay wondered what Gabe thought about what he'd shared.

The young man didn't look bored. And he didn't look judgmental. He looked - Clay felt strange thinking it - safe. He looked like a safe place.

"Did you ever find out what happened to Shadow?"

Clay shook his head. "No. I couldn't stand to think where she might be. Or who might have her. I just had to quit wonderin'."

"What about Evie? I know you saw *her* again."

Clay smiled and nodded. "Not for a few years. She'd gone off to high-school in Dallas. Special school for ballet. My father tole me she'd a said good-bye if she really cared for me. I figured he was right about that."

"Your father was wrong about a lot of things."

"I s'pose." Clay sipped on his mug. Coffee had cooled. He reached for the pot and topped it off.

"Tell me about Evelyn."

Clay studied his boots for a moment before gazing into Gabe's clear brown eyes. "All right, young man. I'll tell you 'bout my Evelyn. I ran into her again on my 18th birthday. One of the worst and best days of my life."

CHAPTER 16

Independence Day

July 10, 1943

Clay flew down the stairs two at a time. Today was the day. He would be free.

Today he was a man.

Eighteen.

He would join the Army. Be with Eric in France. Clay could see himself in his uniform. Saluting his sergeant.

"Happy birthday, Clay," Mama whispered. Her voice sounded brittle, her eyes watery and swollen.

"Thanks, Ma," he kissed her cheek and pulled a chair to the kitchen table.

"Are you going through with it?"

Please be excited with me; he wanted to whoop. But he controlled himself. He would be manly about it. "Yup. Headin' out right after breakfast."

His father wandered into the kitchen in a tee shirt and underwear, his black hair unkempt and tousled. He smelled stale, like old cigarettes and bad wine.

Mama poured Milton a mug of coffee and placed it at his spot at the head of the table. He cupped his big hands around the enameled mug and slurped, his dark eyes languid. "They won't take you."

"Milton!"

He shot her a warning glance. "I'm tellin' him for his own good, Woman. They won't take him. He's too scrawny."

Clay tipped his chin but said nothing. He would return in uniform. He would, with quiet dignity, pack his few things. His father would be surprised.

No. Shocked.

Clay would kiss Mama on the cheek and salute as he departed. His father would shake his head and realize he'd underestimated Clay. All these years.

Once Clay got there - wherever there was - he would have most of his pay sent to Mama. By the time the war was over, she'd be able to leave.

He could see it.

They would get a house together. Keep a garden, some chickens. Safe.

He wrapped the fried egg in a slice of bread and started for the door. "I'll be back this afternoon. In my new duds." He flashed a smile at Mama.

"Don't wreck the truck," his father yelled as the screen door slammed.

•

A dozen other young men sat in a stuffy waiting room at the recruiting station. Overhead fans strained, flipping the magazine pages back and forth. They sat in their dingy skivvies and socks, avoiding eye contact.

Clay stared at the clock on the wall, then at the floor. His dungarees and shirt peeked from under his metal folding chair. He curled his toes to prevent them from poking through his ancient socks. He wished he'd thought about that before now. Maybe borrowed some socks off Eli. Too late now.

A white-robed doctor swept into the room. "Stand please." He perused the group, before jerking his head toward Clay. The trailing nurse smacked her gum and let her eyes travel from his feet to his hair.

She looked unimpressed. "This way please."

He ducked to grab his clothes.

"Leave your things here," she said in a long-suffering twang.

He followed her to a curtained off area with an exam table and sink.

"Someone will be with you." She swished the curtain behind her.

Clay sat on the cold table, swinging his feet, imagining Mama's face when she received the first check. Signed over to her.

The harried looking doctor pushed through the fabric. He held a clipboard with Clay's recruitment form.

"Name?" His tone was no-nonsense.

"Clay Westin."

"Any surgeries?"

"No."

"Illness. Hospitalizations?"

"No." Clay had to drop his eyes.

"Okay, young man. Let's listen." The doctor placed the clipboard on the table and rubbed his stethoscope against his chest to warm it. He smiled in a friendly way as he hunched down and inserted the earpieces.

His eyelids fluttered, and he stared into the corner of the little room, his smile fading.

Clay suddenly heard a clock tick.

The doctor's eyes came back to Clay's – hard. "No illness. Are you certain?" His eyebrows lifted as he stood and removed the stethoscope from his ears. He pushed his chest out and waited, demanding an explanation.

"Just one, one, once," Clay stammered. "Long time ago. I'm all better now."

"You never feel your heart thump extra hard?"

"Sometimes," Clay admitted.

"Well, young man. You've got a grade four heart murmur. No way you'd hold up in combat. And don't waste your government's time trying anywhere else. You've got a defect that'll make them all say no. Your heart's so musical they'll hear you coming down the block." He snickered at his own joke and swished out leaving Clay to slink into the waiting room and dress in front of the remaining hopefuls.

•

Clay turned right into his driveway. He'd driven home slowly hoping some alternative plan would come to him. He'd thought about maybe heading to Dallas. But he had his father's truck. Couldn't steal it. His father would kill him. He would find him and kill him.

A black sedan sped up the driveway from the house, tires firmly in the ruts. Clay swerved off the driveway, hard, barely missing the barbed wire fence. He stopped and watched the vehicle as it continued toward the road, leaving a trail of dust in its wake.

He pulled back onto the driveway toward the house, figuring what to say. To Mama. To his father. He opened the front door quietly. Maybe he could sneak into his room. Not say anything.

Maybe nobody would mention it.

But as he crept toward the stairs, a sound stopped him. Weeping. Mama was sobbing in the kitchen.

He closed his eyes and set his lips. It wasn't that bad. He would get over not making it. He'd find somethin' to do.

Mama sat on the floor, her thin cotton dress spread around her as though she'd collapsed straight down. "Clay! Oh, Clay," her words hiccupped between convulsive gulps for air.

"It's all right, Mama. I'll be okay." He offered his hand to help her rise.

She opened her fist to reveal a crumpled letter. "It's Eric, Clay. He's not coming home. He's ..."

Clay dropped next to her to read the official condolence letter.

The screen door slammed, and Milton staggered in. He looked like he'd been crying - and drinking. His bloodshot eyes were murderous.

"Clay! Off the floor. You look like a dog."

Clay scrambled to rise and met his father in the center of the room. Maybe Clay could distract him. Maybe Mama could escape.

His father grabbed Clay's shirt collar and pulled him close. So close Clay could smell his fermented breath. "You're a shorry excuse for a man," he slurred. He glared over Clay's head. "It's your fault, Pearl. You coddle him. You make him weak."

Clay squeezed his eyes and hunkered into his shoulders, waiting for the hand. But before the hand could fly, and without any warning sensation, Clay's stomach heaved and vomit erupted from him, down the front of his father's shirt.

Milton recoiled and released Clay, his eyes buggy with shock. He pulled his chest in and peeled the stained tee shirt with two fingers.

"Get out!" he pointed the way. "I never want to see your sorry face again."

Clay fled.

• CHAPTER 17 •

Heaven

Clay sprinted a few strides before an excruciating stitch caught up with him. The two-mile driveway would give his father ample time to run him over. He jogged, glancing over his shoulder every few steps. One good side to bein' run over. At least the fearin' would be done.

But what would happen to Mama?

Clay's legs gave out as he approached the road and he crumpled in the ditch. He'd made it. He knew his father would never hurt him where someone else might see.

Eric dead. Mama with him. Alone. He had to stop thinkin'. Or he would go crazy.

He rubbed his temples, stretching the skin back towards his ears, pulling his eyes shut. Where do I go?

West toward Abilene, or east toward town, and Eli's house.

West.

He could not make his legs stop trembling. He'd not eaten since breakfast and probably vomited whatever was left onto his father. He should feel bad about that.

He sighed and forced himself up. He would have liked to march, but all he could manage was a painful shuffle.

He wandered about a mile when he heard the truck behind him. *Knew I should have gone toward town*. He tried to ignore it, just get out of the way, but it screeched to a halt. Clay heard the gears grind as the driver searched for first.

That couldn't be his father. He stopped. Turned carefully. He exhaled. Didn't recognize the truck. It looked new. Sunlight bounced off the windshield, hiding the driver's identity.

The window rolled down. "Clay? Clay Westin? The voice sounded deep and kind.

"Yes, sir?" He shaded his eyes. "Mr. Mayfield?" Clay snapped to attention, then felt stupid.

"You need a ride somewhere, son?"

"No sir," Clay replied automatically. The truck didn't leave so he shrugged, "Got nowhere to go."

"Climb in, son. You can have dinner with us and figure out what to do."

Clay lurched forward. *Us*. He was still thinking about the us when he got to the door. It opened before he could grab the handle. There sat Evelyn Mayfield. Smiling right into him. Those green eyes.

"Well, c'mon. Don't take all day!" Mr. Mayfield grinned.

Clay climbed in next to Evelyn.

They sat so close their legs touched. He flinched at the contact, then slid as close to the door as he could.

It just didn't feel right, sitting so close, feeling her warmth. Clay could smell her hair. A sensation washed over him. He turned his head away, and rolled the window down feeling the wind in his face, so she wouldn't see him thinkin' crazy thoughts.

She still smiled at him - he felt her eyes looking right into the side of his head - until he had to look back. Her gaze was warm and sincere.

"Clay Westin," she declared. "It has been years. Do you remember me?"

"Yeah," he choked, turning back to the window. "I remember you."

Mr. Mayfield turned the truck into the long tree lined driveway.

"You've never seen our house before."

Clay could only shake his head, no.

"You know we are neighbors. My place backs up to your father's, way in the back."

Clay knew.

He'd never seen a house like the Mayfield's. Even in pictures. From the driveway to the doorway, so much grass. Manicured, green and lush. The front of the house had bushes shaped like squares and circles. The walkway was brick, must have been a thousand bricks.

They walked through the front door into a room Evelyn called the foyer. The temperature dropped at least 20 degrees, and Clay rubbed the goose bumps that rose on his thin arms.

"Air conditioning," Mr. Mayfield grinned. "It'll chill you."

Clay nodded, watching his reflection in the black and white marble floor. In the living room, they had varnished wood floors, not dirt, covered with soft, thick rugs with tassels on the ends. Large fans rotated from the ceiling. A marble circular stairway meandered upward like it had all the time in the world.

"Evie," Mr. Mayfield hollered, walking upstairs, "see if Clay would like a shower – and maybe we could find him something to wear while his things get washed."

She led the way. "What size are you?" she glanced over her shoulder.

He shrugged stupidly. "Dunno'. I always get Eric's old clothes."

Eric is dead.

She stopped her feet and faced him. "Wonder if you could wear my pants. You'd slide right out of my father's clothes."

He knew his mouth gaped, but he couldn't help it. "No." He shook his head as hard as he could muster. "I couldn't wear yer clothes. Wouldn't be right."

She nodded and continued down the hall.

"Here is the bathroom, if you'd like to wash up," Evelyn motioned. "I'll get you a towel. Shower runs hot so be careful."

He stood at the doorway to the bathroom, glancing from the shower stall to the hall. He'd never seen a shower. *Was he supposed to go in? What did she want him to do?*

Evie charged back around the corner, bath towel and folded clothing in hand. "Ever used a shower before?"

He could only shake his head, no. She plunked the clothing down on a bench. "Here, I found some jeans and a shirt. They might be big, but they'll do." She started the water for him. "They're not my clothes." She exited, pulling the door firmly behind her.

Clay surveyed the bathroom. Nothin' like the bathroom at school. It smelled of roses and peppermint soap. Plush rug on white tile, yellow floral wallpaper.

He removed his boots and wiggled his dirty toes into the carpet. Tickled. Made him smile.

Steam poured from the shower stall creating comfortable humidity in the small room.

He peeled off his dungarees and checked the water temperature with an outstretched palm. Too hot. He turned the nearest spigot handle away. Too cold. He brought the handle back and stepped in.

Deliciously warm water cascaded over his body, washing him, cleansing him. He lathered his hands with peppermint soap and scrubbed his scalp.

Eric. Gone. Mama.

Soap got into his eyes, and he squeezed tight, raising his face into the pelting stream. Tears began to flow, first from the soap, then from *Eric, Mama, himself. What will happen to me?*

His legs began to shake, and he slid down the cool tile wall of the shower stall until he crouched into the corner, thin arms curled around his legs. He sobbed for - he didn't know how long - until the water began to grow cold.

Get yourself together.

He straightened his cramping legs and let the cool water rush over his face. Bring him back to earth.

Clay stepped from the shower and dried himself. The towel felt like velvet against his skin. The jeans were stiff with newness, the plaid shirt crunchy with starch.

At least they weren't Evie's.

She hadn't brought socks, and Clay stretched his ancient holey socks over his clean, water-shriveled feet. His toes felt oozy and uncomfortable as they scraped against the dirt inside his boots.

He shook his head and sprayed water onto the yellow wallpaper, leaving tiny spots. He winced and used the towel instead.

The mirror over the sink had steamed up bad, so he wiped down the center and blinked at his reflection. His blond hair stuck straight out, like a thatched roof.

Could use a haircut. He looked around for a comb.

He found combs and toothbrushes in a shelf under the sink. He slicked his hair back, tightened his belt, and stepped out into the hallway. The cool air braced him, and he pulled in a lung full.

"Over here, young man," Mr. Mayfield said, from the parlor. "Come, sit down with me. Tell me what's been happening with you."

Clay sank into the leather chair. "What do you mean?"

"It has been seven years since we saw you at the auction. You and your mare. I'll never forget that ride."

"Thank you, sir," Clay hung his head remembering his deal with Mr. Mayfield.

"Whatever happened to that horse?"

"I got sick, couple years back. Almost died. My dad sold her to pay for the hospital."

"Oh, I'm sorry, son. I know that broke your heart." He sounded like he really knew.

"Yessir, it did." Clay studied a tassel just under the toe of his boot. He looked at Mr. Mayfield's face.

Not a hint of condemnation. "I'm sorry I didn't contact you like I promised. I didn't even know until she was already gone..."

The older man waved Clay's apology away. "We haven't seen you back at church." Mr. Mayfield spoke plain. Got straight to it. Clay liked that.

"Yes, sir," Clay looked up. "It's been too long."

"Your father doesn't approve of church, does he?"

That was years ago. "No sir, he doesn't."

"That is his choice. What is your decision about church?"

"I'd like to go sir, now that I'm free." Clay hadn't meant to say free; it just sorta' slipped out.

Mr. Mayfield jiggled his iced tea. The cubes tinkled against the glass. "Tell me about what you do with horses, son."

Clay cleared his throat.

"I'm sorry. Would you like some iced tea?"

"Yes, sir. I would." It seemed okay to say yes.

Now the older man came forward in his chair. He leaned toward Clay.

"Tell me about what you do with horses."

Clay searched Mr. Mayfield's face and saw something real. Something genuine. He wasn't messin' with him. He really wanted to know.

The iced tea magically arrived at his elbow.

Clay sipped, breathed and started. "There's a different way to be with horses, Mr. Mayfield. A way that gets into their hearts. A way that allows them to be the best horse they can be, without ..." he couldn't think of the right word.

"Force?" Mr. Mayfield suggested.

"Yeah! No force, or fear." Clay nodded with vigor.

"So what is this way? I've seen you ride Clay. That day at the auction, I tell you." Mr. Mayfield dropped his open hands, palms up, onto his thighs. "You captured my imagination. I used to watch you with that mare, riding the fence line; no bridle, no saddle." His fingers curled around imaginary reins. "How did you make her do those things?"

"That's just it, sir," Clay answered, feeling his pulse increase. "I didn't *make* her do anything. She wanted to do what I wanted her to do. She wanted to be with me.

"Horses talk to each other, Mr. Mayfield. It's not the same way we talk. Their talk is all in their body. It's about pressure and release. Rhythm and focus. Not words.

"I saw how horses find comfort in each other. In numbers. So I set myself up as Shadow's leader."

"How?" Mr. Mayfield's eyes sparkled.

"It's all about the feet with horses. Whoever moves the feet gets to lead the horse."

"How do you move the feet?"

"It's hard to explain. You gotta' feel for the horse. Figger out how he thinks. All he wants is to be okay. To be safe. And people are the biggest reason horses don't feel okay."

"Why do you say that?" The older man looked skeptical.

"Cause, we catch 'em, sell 'em, use 'em..."

"But they're animals," Mr. Mayfield replied. "That's what they're for. They don't understand."

"They understand more than you think, sir. They know how it feels to be safe, or loved, or used. They *don't* think like we do. But maybe that's why I love 'em so much."

"Can you show me?" Mr. Mayfield's voice was husky with emotion. "We just brought some horses in. They were born on this property, but these are really wild. The ones who have eluded my wranglers for years."

A young man in a starched blue uniform interrupted them. "Sir. What would you like to drink with your dinner?"

Clay had never been called sir. "W ...water," he stuttered.

Mr. Mayfield rose and bowed toward Clay, "after you, young man."

Roast beef, bread, mashed potatoes, and gravy - all in the same meal. As much as anybody wanted. Clay tried not to make a pig of himself, but Evelyn plied him with food until he thought something would rupture.

After apple pie and coffee, they headed outside to look at the new horses. "This one," Mr. Mayfield explained, pointing to a dark bay, alone in a sturdy pen, "is at least six years old. Not had a hand on him except when he was a yearling and was branded and gelded.

We've not been able to catch him, until today. I have a wrangler who says he can break him, but I am concerned, for the man *and* beast."

"Put yourself in the horse's place," Clay said. "Every time he sees a man, hurtful things happen. And now he is separated from everyone he knows, surrounded by, as far as he is concerned, a bunch of lions who want to eat him. This pen feels like death."

Mr. Mayfield shook his head. "Never thought of it from the horse's point of view."

Evelyn smiled as she considered the question.

The gelding watched – on high alert, his head up, eye whites showing. They got too close, and he trotted to the other side of the corral. Their conversation attracted some of Mr. Mayfield's wranglers, outside the main bunkhouse, having a smoke. As soon as they walked over, the horse began moving faster.

But his eyes had that look. The look that says, "please. Please don't hurt me. I just want to live."

Clay slipped through the gate into the pen. His presence was enough to send the bay galloping. Clay allowed him to do his thing. *He is beautiful.*

The horse panicked and tried to leap over the enclosure. The thick cedar posts and boards held. He bounced off, crash-landing onto his side. He flailed for a second then scrambled up and continued his headlong flight. Clay stood quietly in the center of the pen, allowing the horse the freedom to do everything in his power to help himself.

I am your answer. Clay wished the horse could hear his heart. *I am here for you.*

After twenty minutes, the gelding began to slow. His stride became less frantic. He was growing tired. Clay threw his lasso toward the horse's hindquarters. The horse spurted forward.

"I am here with you, no matter what you do, no matter what happens," Clay whispered.

The bay began to flag again, and Clay could see the process taking place within the horse. The gelding fixed his inside ear and eye on Clay.

The horse's eye softened as he realized that Clay had not hurt him. He continued around the man slowing imperceptibly. Clay felt it more than saw it

"That's right," Clay crooned softly. "You're okay. I look like an enemy, but I'm not. You're lookin' for safety. Try me."

The horse slowed to a trot, and the moment he turned his head to focus on Clay with both eyes, Clay exhaled allowing his body to go passive; then he turned and walked away in the opposite direction.

The bay drifted to a soft stop. He watched the man in the center of the corral, his nostrils flaring. He took a tentative step towards Clay, then another. He snorted loud, so loud he scared himself, turned and took off again, tail up, new energy in his stride after the brief rest.

As soon as Clay heard pounding feet, he turned his body, facing the horse again. He added rhythm with the free end of the lasso when the horse slowed.

Clay felt no anger, no impatience. He had done this a hundred times. It always worked. He knew that the horse felt alone without his herd. That the horse *needed* a leader for protection. The horse was convinced that safety lay with the herd.

Clay would allow the horse to prove to himself that Clay was not the problem, Clay was the answer to the problem.

"I will stay with you until you realize I'm *not* your enemy," Clay promised the frightened gelding. "I will stay until you understand that I am the only safety you need. Your herd can't keep you safe. I can and will."

After 15 minutes more the gelding approached the end of his physical desire to flee. He could still run, but running did not appear to deliver him from his predicament. His ear turned in once again as the bay considered the other possibility. Clay could see the horse weighing the choices, including the option that seemed impossible.

The horse was determining whether the man in the center of the pen could be causing his feet to move.

Clay stepped forward, blocking the horse, causing him to turn and whirl away in the other direction. As the bay processed the thought, his tongue came out, licking his lips. His eyes grew soft, and as these physical changes occurred, Clay turned away, relieving the pressure. The bay stopped once more, this time turning to stare at the man.

The horse was not certain how, but it was clear to him that the man was causing the change in his speed and direction. Something only a powerful leader could accomplish. The gelding came forward, just a step, then two. Clay stepped back, matching each step. It gave the horse a flood of relief from his overwhelming fear.

Clay stopped after several steps and allowed the horse to come as near as he wanted. Clay remained still, allowing the horse time to think.

The gelding stayed where he was, but shifted his weight to the front leg farthest from Clay, preparing to flee.

Clay extended his arm, inviting the horse to smell his hand. The horse turned his head away but did not leave. Clay retracted his hand and waited for the horse's eyes to soften again. Waited for the horse to blink. *Wait for the horse to come back to himself.*

Clay extended his hand once more. This time it looked like the gelding couldn't help himself. He had to sniff. Clay felt like he could read the horse's thoughts. *Who is this meat-eater who seems to understand me?*

Clay reached a little higher and rubbed the horse's forehead. The gelding licked his lips again and dropped his head. Clay understood the submission and permission inherent in the signal and stepped forward to scratch the horse gently on the withers, stepping back as the horse relaxed.

Clay stepped forward again.

"Can I touch you here?" Clay asked quietly, more to himself than to the horse. He ran his hand down the gelding's back, to his long tail. The horse drifted away slightly.

Soon he could touch the gelding anywhere he chose. *I want you to want to be with me. I won't force you.* Clay rubbed the big horse, occasionally scratching in a spot he knew would be welcomed.

Clay tossed several loops of his lasso around the thick brown neck.

The horse spooked, opening a gap between Clay and himself. Clay gave the rope a quick tug, stepping backward at the same time. The pressure was released as soon as the horse turned toward Clay. Several pulls and the horse understood how to follow the feel of the rope.

Within minutes Clay could move the horse back and forth in front of him. He touched him all over with firm, gentle strokes, like a mama horse's tongue on a new foal. He knew that the rhythmic pressure of slapping made horses want to leave.

I want you to want to stay with me.

Clay allowed the horse's body to tell him when to continue and when to stop. He knew that every move the horse made, every glance, every flick of the ears or tail, meant something.

He hopped a couple of times, next to the gelding. The horse did not startle. His eyes were soft, his body relaxed.

Clay allowed his belly to gently contact the horse.

No reaction. Still breathing. Still blinking.

I think he's ready.

Clay carefully, his eyes constantly reading the horse, threw his body up onto the back of the bay. He kept his legs together in case he needed a hasty exit.

The horse did not move. Clay slid his leg around and straddled the horse's back. The bay moved slightly. Clay yawned and rubbed the bay's neck. The horse echoed with a sigh and stopped his feet.

Clay climbed off immediately.

Perfect place to stop for the first day.

Only then did Clay notice that every cowhand on the Mayfield Ranch had gathered to see the "bronco busting." They stood silently around the pen, some staring at their feet, some rubbing their noses and sniffling. He found Mr. Mayfield's face, wet with unconsidered tears.

Had he done something wrong?

"Amazing," Mr. Mayfield whispered. "That horse is yours, son. If you want him. I want you to teach all my wranglers to do what you just did.

"I'll pay you $200.00 a month, and you can have your own bunkhouse. Three squares a day, and church on Sunday. How does that sound?" Mr. Mayfield held out his hand for Clay to shake.

More money than Clay had ever dreamed of. A place to live, with horses, near Evelyn. And he would be free from his old man.

He'd died and gone to Heaven.

• CHAPTER 18 •

Home

Clay awoke in his new bed; a real mattress bed, stuffed with cotton, not straw. In his new house. A tiny house - not much more than a room - but his. His own indoor bathroom, with a shower.

He fluffed the downy pillow, burrowing his face into its softness. Clean cotton fragrance filled his senses. Overnight it seemed, his luck had changed.

Luck?

No. Not luck. God. God was finally smiling on him. "Thank you," Clay whispered into the pillow. He was clean and free. His whole life ahead.

Mama and Eric. Their faces intruded into his happiness. He did not know what to do with them.

A thump on the door pulled his attention back to reality before the grieving could start.

"Breakfast at the big house. Come and get it!" The thumping and the call continued down the row of bunkhouses.

He scrambled out of bed, pulled on his new dungarees and shirt. Old boots.

He'd have to ask Mr. Mayfield for a ride into town. Get a few things. Underwear, socks, a hat. He'd left his hat at home. *Not home anymore. This is my home.*

He raced up to the big house, spurred on by hunger pangs.

A short line at the back door helped Clay know where to go. Bacon. He could smell it. A table covered with large platters of food lay before him. The ten other wranglers jabbered and helped themselves to eggs, bacon, sausage and headed to a second table, surrounded by chairs. A red and white gingham cloth covered the eating table, and blue enamel pots full of coffee stood in the center.

Clay snatched a plate and began piling on eggs. A stream of saliva dribbled onto his chest. He wiped his mouth with his sleeve, glancing around to see if anyone had observed.

He found a spot next to a young wrangler who introduced himself as Jake.

"Where'd you learn that stuff?"

"What stuff?" Clay asked, out of one side of his mouthful of the creamiest, richest scrambled eggs he'd ever tasted. He shook a little salt and pepper. Perfection.

Jake crammed a sausage link in his already full mouth and didn't bother to hide it. "That horse stuff."

Clay's head remained bowed over his plate in a serious eating position. He glanced at Jake sideways, "I learnt from watching my father's horses."

"Who's your father?"

"Milton Westin."

Jake stopped chewing and sat up, his mouth wide, a slurry of yellow eggs and brown meat moving with his tongue. Clay had to look away.

"You're Milton Westin's son?" He ripped a bite from his toast. "You don't look like him."

Dang it. His appetite vanished. The eggs and bacon pointless.

"Yea', I know. You don't have ta' shout it."

"Sorry," Jake shrugged. "Ya' gonna' eat that?"

"Nah. You can have it." Clay pushed his plate over and rose. "Gonna' go talk to Mr. Mayfield."

"Stay away from his daughter. He's real pertective ..."

Clay shrugged and walked outside, around to the front of the house.

Evie answered the door. "Good morning Clay." Her full lips parted and her smile. Her smile. He stood, unable to pull his eyes from her mouth.

She lifted her eyebrows and one cheek dimpled. "GOOD MORNING CLAY." She didn't shout, it was more like a play shout, with lots of air in the words.

"Uh." He could not think why he had knocked on the door.

She backed up, invited him in. He followed meekly. Wished he had a hat to hang onto. He wasn't sure what to do with his hands.

"Can I talk to yer dad?"

"Right this way, sir."

"Clay," Mr. Mayfield sounded excited to see him. "How did you sleep?"

"Great," he replied, meaning it.

"Need anything?"

"Yes, yes sir." He remembered now. "I need some things from town. Hat, socks... things." He glanced sideways.

"Evie can take you." Mr. Mayfield turned to confirm with her. "Right?"

She laughed. "I'd love to."

And that was that. He was on his way to town, with Evelyn Mayfield driving her father's new truck.

She drove a mite faster than Clay would have. She glanced over. "How's that brake working for you?"

He relaxed his tense foot and slouched. "Not worth a darn." He grinned.

She grinned back and pressed the gas pedal harder. They roared down the dirt road, truck fishtailing. Clay willed his feet to stay where they were. If he had to die, this was as good a way as any.

"Any chance you could help me with my mare?"

"Shore," he replied, surprised. "Didn't know you had a horse."

"Daddy bought her. She's a really nice mare. She's just not so nice – if you know what I mean."

"No, I don't know. Tell me."

"Well, she bites." Ev crinkled her perfect nose. "And she's cinchy. And sometimes..."

He could not drag his eyes away from her lips, the way her teeth peeked through when she said certain words.

"... She runs over me when I'm leading her. Other than that she's perfect." Evie stopped talking and stared at him. "Are you listening to me?"

Clay nodded. "Hmm. Perfect. You'll have to show me. If we survive the trip to town."

"Deal," she laughed. Three light, lovely, musical notes, from high to low. Clay had never heard anything more beautiful.

It took him a moment to realize; he was smiling. He couldn't seem to stop, so he rolled down the window and watched the ditch roll by.

•

Evelyn's black mare pinned her ears and stuck her nose into the far corner of the box stall. She swished her long tail and shifted her weight from one hind foot to the other. Evie opened the stall door and stepped in.

"I wouldn't go in there," Clay cautioned.

"She always does this," Evie replied but stopped.

"That mare is warning you. If she kicks, you shouldn't be surprised."

Evie huffed and backed out, closing the latch. "What should I do then? If I don't grab her, I'll never get to ride."

"That's the first thing." Clay replied. "You need to decide right now, is it performance you want, or relationship? If alls you want is performance, I'm not your guy. That's what my father does.

"If you want relationship, well. Once your horse knows you are for her – you two will be able to do anythin'."

Evelyn's head rocked back with surprise. "Don't I have a relationship with her already? She's mine. I feed her, give her carrots. What else can I do?"

"Right now your relationship is all about you. What your mare can do for *you*. She needs to know that you are all about her. That she means more to you than any ride. Do you really want to ride so bad you'd force her?" He raised his eyebrows.

She blinked. "I never thought about it that way." Evie gazed at her mare. "How do I get her to want me? How do I tell her I love her?"

He laughed. "It's all about the feet."

Evie shrugged and pushed the halter into his chest. "Okay, mama horse. Show me."

Clay knelt and picked up a handful of tiny stones. "Here," he handed Evie several. "Hold these."

He focused hard on the mare's tail. Found a single hair and stared. He lightly tossed one pebble at the mare's tail. It touched that one hair and she jumped forward banging her nose into the corner. She turned her head, eyes wide, ears forward.

Clay relaxed his body. "Oh, hello."

The mare flattened her ears and glared at him for a moment before returning her head to the corner. She slashed her tail to let him know she meant it.

He tossed another stone. Very light. Barely touched her. The mare snorted and whirled about, head high, eyes bulging.

"Hello again."

Evie sat and watched from a hay bale, legs crossed, an amused smile on her face.

Clay waited.

The mare returned to her corner, but her expression had changed, and she did not take her left eye off Clay. He prepared to toss one last tiny rock, but the mare turned around came to the door, ears forward, all friendly like.

Evie's head tilted, and she jumped up. "What in the world? How did you make her do that?"

"Didn't *make* her do anything. Once she knew I could touch her from far away, and I could touch her, but I wasn't hurtin' her, well, she got curious. Now she wants to know more."

He placed the halter on the mare's head and handed the rope to Evie. "Shall we?"

She led the mare through the aisle to the paddock.

Clay grabbed a saddle and swung it onto the top rail of the fence. "You say she's cinchy. Show me what she does."

Evie started to tie the mare to the fence.

"Why are you tyin' her?"

She stopped and handed him the rope. "I guess I'm not. Show me what I should do."

Clay placed the rope over her elbow. "Hold it over your arm. Like that."

"And then?" she inquired sweetly.

"And then show me how you saddle her."

"Jake always saddles her. I can't even lift this heavy old thing."

Clay took the lead rope, slid the saddle blanket in place and in one graceful arc swung the saddle onto the gleaming back.

"That's different," Evie observed.

"Yup." He snugged the cinch but didn't make it tight. He held the lead rope in his left hand and twirled the tail of the rope with his right. The mare walked a few steps around him and stopped.

Clay snugged the cinch again and asked the mare to go in the opposite direction. This time he added a little more speed in the twirl and the mare jogged. He jogged with her, and she stopped after a few feet.

He snugged the cinch a last time.

He spread his hands. "Doesn't seem cinchy to me."

Evie marched over, hands on her slim hips. "Me neither. Now what, cowboy?"

"Now, we need to teach her to come pick you up. It's not a good idea to get on a horse who doesn't want you up there."

Clay showed Evelyn how to focus on the part of the horse you wanted to go away, how to soften her body to draw the mare to her, how to use rhythm to create pressure, release to reward.

After an hour, Evelyn could invite her mare to pick her up from the fence. No biting, no bucking, no resistance.

"It's like a miracle, Clay." She pushed damp hair from her face, her tiny nose covered in sweaty beads of victory. "I can't believe this is the same horse." She rubbed the mare's neck.

"Your horse can't believe you're the same person," Clay replied. "This is a good place to stop."

Evelyn hopped down, and they meandered to the barn, the mare between them.

As they headed back to the house, Evie tucked her arm into his.

He stopped. Glanced sideways at her. Her smile dizzied him, and he had to plant his feet.

"Are you okay?" She slid her arm from his and clutched at him.

He was gonna' faint. Mortified. Had to put his head down. "It's my heart," he coughed. "It doesn't always work right." He closed his eyes and straightened.

She stepped in front of him, her face serious. "Clay Westin. You have the best heart I've ever seen."

He could only smile foolishly and lean against the barn, thumping his chest. He regained his composure. "I'm okay now."

But he had lied.

He couldn't eat or sleep for two days. And he couldn't stop looking at his arm, where she held him.

• CHAPTER 19 •

Picnic

Clay slipped the saddle off his dark bay gelding. The horse had come along quick in six weeks. Greeted Clay at the gate. Knew how to move off a leg, stay on a cow, and raise a cloud sliding to a stop. Ready to start workin' cattle.

Half of Mr. Mayfield's wranglers had quit along the way. Clay felt bad about that, but Mr. Mayfield kept telling him it was all right. "It's their choice, son."

The five who remained were easy to work with. They seemed real interested in knowing about horses, and how to really *be* with them. Not just use them.

Clay slapped the saddle over the stall door, just as Evie appeared.

"Hey there," Evie said, leaning over the stall door, smiling right into him.

"I'm sorry ... didn't see you."

"It's all right," her wide-set eyes twinkled with mischief. "Have you had lunch yet?"

He knew that she knew that he hadn't. But he played along.

"Nope, not yet."

"Would you like to picnic?"

His heart fluttered. "With you?"

"With me," she nodded.

He closed his eyes and breathed her air. "I'd love to."

"Yay!" She clapped her hands and lifted the brown paper bag. "We've got chicken salad and lemonade."

•

Sam Mayfield scratched his ear as he watched Clay and Evie from his Palladian window in the study.

The boy was a peculiar combination of traits. He'd never met anyone so transparent and guarded at the same time. Clay's competence with horses was miraculous, nothing less. And he could talk - about horses. Any other topic and the boy could hardly scratch two words together.

Clay seemed unable to hide his thoughts - particularly about Evelyn, but mention his family, and the boy's face slammed shut. He suspected a great deal of pain lived inside of Clay.

He'd met Milton, more than once. Seen him in action at the Saturday auctions. Seemed a small miracle that Clay had escaped.

It pleased Sam to have the boy here. And he hoped it pleased God too. He could make a difference. Help Clay get started in life. Especially since Evelyn had made her feelings known.

Sam shook his head at the unpredictability of love. He'd fallen in love with an unlikely woman. It made sense that Katya's daughter would see something special in an unlikely boy. Sam's job was to support Evie by supporting Clay. He'd see to it his daughter was taken care of.

He reached for the picture of Katya on his desk and ran his finger around the gold frame. He fell for her the first time he saw her dance with the Ballet Russe. She never starred in a ballet. She was just one of the many. But not to him. He loved her. And convinced her to marry him. She defected, given up her mother country, for love.

She was so young when the cancer took her.

Sam sighed and placed the picture tenderly on the desk.

He couldn't wait to see what Clay would do with the next batch of horses.

Sam rose and went downstairs.

•

Evie handed Clay the paper bag. Clay saddled Evie's mare and tucked the lunch into his own saddle pack. He offered his knee as a mounting block and hoped he didn't wince. She was lighter than he expected - delightfully so - and she floated up and onto the mare's back. "Thank you, kind sir," she said slipping her feet into the stirrups.

Clay, still on bended knee, gazed up into her face. His smile went deeper; to a place he'd never felt. He could not have not smiled.

He placed his hand on her foot. She felt small and fragile and warm. Her eyes followed his, and in her eyes, he'd found his home. He didn't know how else to describe it. When she was with him, his heart was home.

Evie offered her hand, her red hair falling forward into her face as she leaned over. She giggled, "may I help you?"

He accepted and held on to her hand for a moment longer than necessary. She blushed and sat upright, tucking her hair behind her ear.

"Are we going to picnic or aren't we? It's getting hot." She tried to look stern, but the deep dimple and laughing eyes gave her away.

"Yes ma'am," he saluted. He swung up onto his gelding, and they headed toward the creek where the trees made for cool shade – even in August.

Clay unrolled the thick blanket he'd brought and they sat cross-legged, taking small, careful bites, sending shy glances to each other.

"Clay?"

"Yes."

"What do you want from your life?"

He stopped chewing.

Stumped.

Heat rushed to his face as he tried to formulate an answer. What if he answered wrong? *What was she looking for?* He took a swig of lemonade, buying time.

But it didn't help.

He shrugged. "I ... I don't know."

Her smile did not change. She leaned forward and rested her small hand on his.

Warm, soft.

He scrutinized the blanket, unable to meet her gaze.

"I mean - what do *you* want?" Her voice was so gentle, so safe he could think again.

All he wanted was her. His face relaxed, and he breathed in, closing his eyes briefly.

Lavender lingered in the air.

He wrapped her small hand in both of his.

He had to tell her, and he gazed into her eyes. He hadn't noticed before how the green and gray of her eye softened and grew lighter as the colors melded away from the center, and then the emerald green-ness of the very edge of her iris. He'd never noticed that before.

He was compelled to speak the truth. "All I want is you, Evie."

She tucked her head into her shoulder and dimpled. "Do you know what I want?"

He shrugged and blinked, his heart thudding. He was at her mercy.

"I want to watch you dance with horses for the rest of my life."

Clay's hands melted into the blanket, and he couldn't find them.

Unworthiness reared up and fear trickled down the back of his neck.

Why would she want that?

But when he gazed into her eyes, he had to believe.

He found his hands.

They touched her face, and she leaned into him.

His lips found hers. And he knew he would never be the same.

•

Three weeks later, Clay paced around his tiny house, heart palpitating as he rehearsed his speech. "Mr. Mayfield, sir. I would like to ask for your daughter's hand in marriage."

No. Sounded stupid.

"Mr. Mayfield. Evelyn and I would like to marry."

No. He didn't actually know if Ev wanted to marry him.

What if she changed her mind?

What if she found out? Discovered who he really was.

He practiced in the mirror. "Evening sir, I'd like to ask your permission ..." His eyes looked terrified even to himself.

What if he says no?

Clay combed through his hair.

Took a breath and headed out.

His hands shook as he knocked at the door of the main house. He'd bought a suit. Navy blue. The tailor had stuck a handkerchief in the breast pocket.

Should he leave it or take it out?

Might need it.

Might start sweatin'.

He straightened his tie and cleared his throat as Mr. Mayfield opened the door. All six foot three – looking down.

Looking surprised.

"Well, Clay. How are you?"

"I'm fine, sir. How are you?"

"Come in! Why are you so dressed ...?"

Clay saw the dawning on Sam Mayfield's face even before he finished the sentence. "Let's go in the office, young man." He led the way, closing the doors behind them.

He strolled to his desk and sat, waving Clay to the chair facing the desk. "Have a seat Clay and tell me, what's on your mind tonight?"

Clay's knees gave out, and he was glad for the soft cushion of the chair.

"Sir." Clay's throat closed, and he swallowed hard.

Dang.

He rubbed his palms against his thighs. He was gonna' rub a hole in his new pants. "Sir I'd like to ask Evie to marry me."

The words tumbled out so fast Clay feared he would need to repeat them.

But Mr. Mayfield did not seem surprised. He rubbed his chin, nodding slowly. "Do you have a ring?"

"No, not yet. I wanted to ask you first." He wished he'd brought his hat; he couldn't seem to stop clasping and unclasping his hands. It was like they had minds of their own.

"I appreciate that." Mr. Mayfield rose and sauntered toward the door. "Stay here son. I have something I'd like to show you,"

He returned shortly with a small black velvet box.

Clay rose, unable to sit any longer. Mr. Mayfield carefully opened the box to reveal an exquisite gold ring with a large tear shaped sapphire in the center. The center stone was surrounded by diamonds and smaller sapphires.

Mr. Mayfield handed the box to Clay who held it carefully. He had to sit. He was befuddled and looked into the older man's face.

Sam Mayfield stared at the ring, his eyes glistening. "This was Katya's - my wife's - engagement ring.

"I saved it for Evie. I don't know if you want it, or if you'd like to take it and change the setting. I'm sure Ken in town could help you."

"You're just givin' this to me?"

"If you want it, son. If you'd like to get your own ring, I understand."

"What do you think Evie would like?"

Sam Mayfield chuckled, his voice husky and low. "That - young man - is now your problem."

Clay did not sleep. About every fifteen minutes, he'd flick on the light, open the box and stare at the most beautiful ring he'd ever seen. He'd close the box, turn out the light and lay there until he couldn't stand it and had to look again.

The next morning Clay raced through his chores. He wanted a shower before their picnic. He wanted his hair clean and his breath fresh.

They met at the barn. Clay had the horses ready. Evie handed him the brown bag with sandwiches and lemonade. He patted his pocket. Still there.

He led the black mare to the aisle and dropped the reins. Ev approached, and Clay pulled the box from his pocket. He dropped onto one knee, balancing the box on the other.

His face grew hot, and his eyes stung, but he continued. "Evelyn Mayfield. Will you marry me?"

Her quick inhalation and delighted expression lifted him to his feet. She threw her arms around him, burrowing her face into his neck.

"Yes!" she breathed. "Yes."

He backed her up and knelt again, slipping the ring onto her slim finger. She held up her hand to admire.

"It was your mother's."

"I know." She pulled him up and gazed at it again. "Oh Clay, I love it."

He kissed her gently on the mouth. Her warmth. She vibrated with life.

He stepped back, feeling supremely content. "Shall we picnic?"

"Yes!" she gushed. "Let's picnic."

•

Clay helped her down and tethered the horses. Evie smoothed out the blanket and unwrapped the sandwiches. Clay plopped down and inhaled.

It felt good to be alive.

"Am I ever going to meet your parents?" Evie asked softly.

Clay stopped chewing.

"Um. Yes?" A sharp twinge of guilt stabbed his joy.

He had not even thought about Mama once.

What kind of a son are you?

"When, Clay?"

"Soon."

Evie sat straighter. "I think it would be good to meet them this week. I want to see your mother's beautiful face again."

Clay smiled. His mother was beautiful. He'd never heard anyone say it, but it was true.

He'd have to tell her. Next time he saw her, he would.

A thought hit him. That could work.

"How 'bout Saturday? After lunch?" *While my father is at the auction.*

She seemed satisfied. "It's a date."

• CHAPTER 20 •

Pearl

Pearl knew she was dying. Her body had stopped making water. She had no more tears and was too weak to get herself anything. She'd cried out for help the first couple days, but Milton was either too drunk to hear, or gone.

Her jaw had throbbed like no pain she'd ever felt before, but now even that ache was ebbing.

She dearly wanted to see Clay.

See if he'd really found his calling, like the rumors she'd heard from Milton.

Weeks ago Milton stormed in for supper. Angry as a snake. Some of his friends had worked for Mr. Mayfield. *Had worked.* Clay's presence caused quite a split.

Some of the wranglers couldn't stomach a kid coming in and showing them up.

And they didn't mind complaining to Milton about his son. And Milton didn't mind complaining to her.

Pearl had turned away. Started washing the dishes. She didn't want him to see the light in her eyes. Afraid she might giggle out loud.

She splashed about in the sink and smiled to herself.

It had to be true. Milton would not make up a story like that. She'd placed her hand over her heart, long fingers patting gently. It was worth it. Every minute of it.

But that was weeks ago. Now she was coming to the end. The doctor pulled the abscessed tooth last week, but she could still feel infection eating through her jawbone.

She'd complained once to Milton, but he wouldn't take her back. Too costly.

A few days of not eating left her unable to rise, even to the outhouse. She was mortified at first but now, well, no need to worry about that.

She just wanted to see Clay.

Touch his face.

You will see him again.

•

Clay pulled up in front of his father's house. The truck was gone. Good sign.

The place looked run down, like nobody had cared about it for a while. Weeds in Mama's flowerbed and sawgrass in the garden. The tomato plants were loaded, with rotten fruit on the ground.

Not like Mama.

Dandelions shoved through the bricks in the walkway. Clay bent down and pulled one up.

It was real quiet.

Clay approached the back door. “Hello,” he hollered. Didn’t feel right just walkin’ in.

Silence.

His heart began to bang against his ribs. An ache of dread filled him as he opened the back door. “Mama?”

He held the door for Evie. She glanced at him, her nostrils flaring. He could smell it too.

Smelled like sickness.

Clay stood a moment longer, then raced to the bedroom door.

Clay turned the doorknob, his heart pounding hard. He walked through the doorway in a crouched position. He felt out of place - an intruder.

Evie stayed close to his back.

“Mama,” he called softly.

He could hear her ragged breathing. The stuffy room reeked of disease.

And old pee.

Clay's hand flew to his mouth, covering his nose. He turned to Evie.

"Open the window," he choked. "We gotta' get some air in here. Mama," he called again, a little louder.

As the light filled the room, Clay saw her. She lay on her left side in a fetal position. Her long silvery hair, greasy and matted, clung to her head and neck.

Clay sat on the edge of the bed and touched her back. Every vertebra protruded through her dirty nightgown. He swallowed hard. No time to wonder.

She needed help.

"Mama, I'm here," he said, his voice low.

She struggled to roll over and mumbled something. She tried to reach for him, but her thin arms fell back onto her chest. "Wa"

Clay understood. "Evie, she needs water."

Evie spun around and took off for the kitchen.

Clay took her in his arms, and Evie held the cup of water to her cracked lips.

Mama swallowed a couple of sips. "Thank you," she rasped, taking Evie's hand. She leaned into Clay, her fever soaking through his shirt.

"Mama, you need the doctor."

"No Clay. I just needed to see you again." She smiled and closed her eyes. "Let me rest here a bit."

He placed her gently on her side. She breathed out with effort and blinked into the brightness. "I'm glad to see the sun."

Clay caught Evie's eye. They had to get her out of here. His father would be home soon, and Mama needed care. He motioned his head toward the door and Ev nodded in agreement.

"Mama, we're takin' you with us. To Mayfield's"

She didn't argue. "I'll go. But help me get cleaned up first. Would you run a bath for me? I believe it would make me feel better."

Clay ran the water and carried Mama into the tub.

She weighed nothin'.

He stripped the sheets on the bed and listened to Evelyn bathe Mama.

"These need to be burned," he muttered and wondered where his father had been sleeping. Surely not in the filthy bed.

Clay stretched the clean sheets on the bed relieved that she'd agreed to go with them. They would head into town first. See the doc.

They wrapped her up in a towel and Evelyn got her into a cotton dress. Mama's wrists looked like little toothpicks protruding from the sleeves. Clay stared at the blue veins in her hands. Hands that rubbed his back, made his meals, cared for him.

"Thank you," Mama said. "I do feel better now."

Evelyn stroked Mama's face gently bringing the wet hair out of her eyes and mouth. Her blue eyes had shrunk back into her head, dark bruised looking circles under them. Her skin looked translucent, withered and dry.

She looked so old.

I can't believe it's only been a few months.

"Clay, would you make me some tea?"

Mama's tea.

He nodded and headed to the kitchen. He filled the kettle and turned the flame on high. She liked her tea from a porcelain cup. The cup sat next to the matching teapot. They had always been there.

He glanced out the window. No sign of his father's truck.

Clay poked his head back into the bedroom. Smelled better.

"Evelyn, will you brush my hair?"

Something in Mama's tone made Clay turn his head and walk back into the kitchen.

Didn't want to cry in front of her.

Beautiful face. Evie's words came to him, and he remembered his wanting to tell Mama how beautiful she was.

Didn't want to forget.

He started back to the bedroom while it was on his mind. He'd hold her hand and tell her. But the whistle of the kettle called Clay back to the kitchen.

He found the tea strainer and loose tea. He spooned the tiny fragrant leaves into her porcelain teapot and poured the water. Steam rose, tickling his nostrils. Clay added a teaspoon of sugar to the teacup, then poured the brew through the strainer.

He looked through the window. No truck.

He started back to the bedroom carefully balancing the delicate cup.

"Clay!" Evelyn called. It was a strange, choky call.

Clay heard the urgency and tried to hurry. The little cup clattered against the saucer as he walked faster.

"Clay!" It was louder this time and panicky.

He took a huge stride.

Evelyn sat there, eyes huge, holding Mama's hand.

Mama was gone. Her jaw slack, eyes vacant.

The lace curtains blew out suddenly as if she'd left on the breeze.

He dropped the cup and hot tea splattered against his pants leg, burning his ankles. He raced to the kitchen, fingers trembling. *Stupid. Stupid! Shoulda' called the doctor right away. As soon as I saw her...*

The operator answered.

"Dr. Porter," Clay gasped.

"Home or office?"

Clay had to think. Saturday. "Home!"

The phone rang twice before the doctor answered.

"Dr. Porter? It's Clay Westin. My mama's real sick. We need you right away."

He spat the words out quick and slapped his hand over his mouth.

Don't lose it. Keep it together.

"What's the matter with her?"

Clay heard weeping from the bedroom and had to lean into the wall. He clutched the phone and closed his eyes.

He could hear the blood swooshing through his veins.

"I think she's gone." He hated how small and whiny his voice sounded.

"I'm on my way, young man," Dr. Porter replied quietly.

Evelyn sat on the chair on the front porch, Clay on the steps, head in his hands.

They heard the tires first. Clay glanced at Evie.

They rose together to greet the doctor.

But it was Milton. He drove past them, arm out of the window in a jovial wave.

The hairs rose on Clay's neck. He tried to prepare himself.

The old truck lurched to a halt under the pecan tree, and Milton tipped out unsteadily.

He's drunk.

"Clay!" his father stumbled closer. "Let me meet yer young lady!"

Evelyn stepped forward as he approached. "Hello, Mr. Westin," she said somberly reaching out to shake his hand.

"Gawd, she's sherious," Milton winked at Clay. "Where'd you find someone sho ... depressin'?"

I hate him.

Clay glanced at Evelyn and his heart filled with admiration. She did not crumble; she raised one eyebrow, released Milton's hand and stepped back. "It is nice to meet you," was all she said.

"What is wrong wish you people? You look like shomeone's died!" his father slurred.

"Dad, I need to tell you something..."

A vehicle pulled up the driveway and distracted Milton. Doctor Porter parked and climbed from his black sedan.

"What the? What's the doc doin' here?"

"I called him," Clay replied. "I didn't know what else to do."

"Who will pay?" his father's voice changed. "It's not cheap to get the doc out here."

"I will, Dad," Clay replied. "I have money."

"You do?" His father's face lit up, "How much ya' got? Lend me a buck?"

"Dad," Clay wanted to kick him. "Mama is gone." His chin quivered, and he braced it with his hand. "I called the doctor because Mama is dead."

The sheriff pulled in followed by Mr. Mayfield.

Milton stared at the growing number of cars in his front yard, and suddenly collapsed, legs straight out in front of him. He shook his head, looking confused. His voice was soft. "She's gone? She has been feelin' poorly. I didn't think she would die." He glared at Clay. "What did you do to her?"

Milton lurched onto his hands and knees, crawling for two steps before scrambling to his feet. "What did you do?" he screamed and stumbled into the house.

Mr. Mayfield approached Clay and Evelyn. "I'm sorry, son," he said softly, offering Clay his hand.

"Thank you," he replied. "Thank you for everything..."

"She is in a better place now Clay," Mr. Mayfield said.

Clay could only nod, trying to imagine what kind of a place that might be.

A cold pressure filled his chest. The ground? Where do people go when they die? Do they simply cease?

"Would you take Ev home with you?" Clay asked. He did not want her subjected to any more.

Evelyn stared at him in disbelief. "I want to stay here. I will stay with you until this is done," she stuck her chin out.

Mr. Mayfield smiled at Clay. "Better let her do what she wants."

"Yessir," Clay answered, putting his arm around her slim waist. She sidled even closer. He could smell her hair...

You will lose her.

He could see it. His mind whirled with the hideous vision. Someday someone would say, "I'm sorry. Your Evelyn is gone."

Clay pulled himself away from her. "Oh, God," he cried.

"What? Clay what is it?" she followed him.

"I am going to lose you," he gasped.

"Clay," she declared, looking into his eyes. "You can't lose me."

"What about death?" he demanded.

"Death cannot part us," she said. "We belong to Jesus. He has overcome Death."

I hope you are right, he thought, watching the doctor and sheriff carry the sheet-covered stretcher to the ambulance.

Oh, I hope you are right.

• CHAPTER 21 •

Married

October 13,1944

Clay held Evelyn's hand as they stood before Mr. Mayfield and the pastor at the front of the church. She squeezed his arm and pressed closer.

"Tomorrow morning, 10:00 sharp, meet me here." Her breath smelled like cinnamon, and she had a tiny bit of brown powder on her chin. He wiped it off with his thumb.

She grinned and wiped again with her hand. "I made some snickerdoodles. For our trip. I guess I'm wearing them too."

"They smell divine."

"Tomorrow."

They'd rented the whole place at Ronnie's Cafe. It was a casual family style restaurant, but tonight they had laid out the silver, china, and white linen.

Clay pulled Evie's seat out for her and then sat in his own. She handed him a package. "Your wedding gift."

He stared at it a moment, then looked around the table at the wedding party. "Open it." Eli Jensen said, with authority.

"Yes, Clay. Open it, open it!" Evie echoed.

It was a brown leather Bible. Clay David Westin engraved in the bottom right corner.

He lifted the cover.

She had written her name and the date.

"I never had a Bible of my own."

He ran his fingers over his name on the cover. He liked the way they felt.

"I figured," she said.

"Thank you; I love it."

He handed her a small package and watched her every move. Her eyes sparkled, and she smiled at him as she ripped the silver paper.

"Oh, Clay," her eyes went soft and shimmery. "They're beautiful."

She pulled the black leather gloves onto her long fingers. "So soft."

She rubbed the back of her gloved hand against her cheek. "I will wear them to the ballet."

He liked the thought of that.

•

The next day Clay stood in front of the full length mirror in a black tuxedo.

He'd never even seen a tuxedo before. But Evie had picked it out, and he could still smell her perfume on his lapel.

He brought the fabric to his nose and breathed it in. His eyes closed as he focused on the fragrance of her.

In an hour he would stand in front of God and man and exchange vows with Evelyn.

His Evelyn.

Mama, I wish you were here to see this.

They would drive to Austin, spend the night, then on to Galveston. To the Hotel Galvez.

For a week.

Alone.

Together.

He felt queasy, but it wasn't unpleasant. The thought of being with her *that way* made him warm and tingly all over.

Will my father show up?

They had sent an invitation but received no reply. It would be easier if he didn't.

Evie really wanted him there.

But Clay knew. Knew that if his father came, so would trouble. *God, I just want this day to be perfect. For her.*

"Clay! You all right in there?" Mr. Mayfield slipped through the front door of Clay's little bunkhouse.

"Yessir, I'm fine," he reached out to shake hands.

Samuel Mayfield pulled Clay into his chest and thumped Clay's back until he coughed. "Please. Please call me Dad, not sir," he said, opening his arms. "I want to tell you something. Can we sit a moment?"

"Sure." Clay's knees collapsed onto his neatly made bed.

"Do you remember that Christmas?"

Clay smiled. "Of course. I met you and Evie that day."

Sam nodded. "We prayed for you starting *that day*."

"We who?" Clay asked feeling confused.

"Evie and me. God told her to pray for you. I just wanted to let you know how proud I am of you ... of how far you've come."

"Thank you, sir, I mean, Dad." Tears pounded behind his eyes.

Sam Mayfield took out his handkerchief and blew his nose. He reached back into his pocket and pulled out a set of keys. "Here. These fit the Buick out front. I've already filled it with gas, and if you'll give me your suitcase, I'll pack it in *your* car."

Clay's mouth flopped open.

"The only thing I ask of you, son ..."

"Yes?"

"The only thing I ask is that you take care of her. Love her. Protect her."

"I promise, sir - I'm sorry. I mean, Dad. I promise."

"Good. Now let's go. Don't want to be late to your own wedding!"

•

It seemed to Clay as though he walked down the aisle, said, "I do" and then ate cake. He couldn't remember many details of the day.

Except, that moment at the front of the church, when he began to fear he may vomit, and the organ played *Handel's Water Music,* and he turned to look.

And his knees went weak. She was there.

She had Bluebells and tiny white flowers in her hair.

She promised to love him forever. No matter what happened to them.

And then they were pelted with rice and herded to the fellowship hall .

And then dancin' with Evie. He'd never forget that.

They fit perfectly. Their noses fit, her lips fit his.

Their bodies aligned perfectly.

He held her close and could feel her heart against his chest. She buried her face in his neck, and he felt her warm breath.

He could have stayed that way forever.

But the song ended. And Sam Mayfield wanted a dance with his daughter.

The next thing Clay knew they changed into travelling clothes, and loaded into the Buick.

Evie laughed and unfolded the map as Clay settled into the five-hour drive to Austin.

"You hungry?" he asked.

She stared at him. "Clay, we just had cake and roast beef and ham biscuits."

"I'm not sayin' I'm hungry. I'm wonderin' if you are."

She reached for his hand. "No, Mr. Westin. I am not hungry right now."

Clay pulled the car over to the side of the road.

"What are you doing?"

"I want to kiss the new Mrs. Westin," Clay said, leaning over.

"By all means, Mr. Westin."

•

They pulled up at the front of the Hotel.

A young man in a black uniform stepped forward to open the Buick door. "Welcome to the Hotel Blue Bell," he chimed. Clay grinned and glanced at Evie.

Three porters converged to pull their suitcases from the car. Clay stood by, attempting to assist.

Evie grabbed his hand and whispered into his ear, "we need to check in. This way," and she pulled Clay into the lobby, towards the desk.

"May I help you, sir?" The slim, blonde receptionist asked brightly, glancing towards the front door and the Buick. She seemed pleased by what she saw and rested her blue eyes on Clay. "Your name, sir?"

"Uh. Westin, Mr. and Mrs."

She ran her long red fingernail down the guestbook. "Ah, yes." Her eyebrows flicked upwards momentarily, "the honeymoon suite." She hit the t hard and let the ah linger.

"Enjoy your stay." She dropped the keys into the waiting hand of a young, heavyset porter.

"This way, sir and madam," the porter invited in a smooth baritone. "Elevators"

He held the doors open for Clay and Evie, then hit the illuminated button for the tenth floor. The doors closed with a pneumatic hiss.

"Clay followed Ev into the corner of the elevator, feeling confused. "Why are we in this closet?" he whispered in her ear.

"It's not a closet," Evie whispered back. "It's an elevator. It's taking us to our room."

"How?"

The elevator lurched and rocked Clay back against the wall. He gripped her hand and stared at Evie.

"It's OK," she whispered. "They all do that."

The porter kept his eyes locked on the door.

It seemed like a very long ride. Clay couldn't wait to get off the thing.

They trundled to the end of the hall.

"Here we are." The porter fumbled with the keys, then threw back the door. "Honeymoon Suite."

"Stay there Ev. I want to carry you across the threshold."

"Really?" she wrinkled her nose doubtfully.

Clay followed the porter as he unloaded their bags and placed them in the closet. He turned and stood for a moment, directly in front of Clay, palm outstretched, face impassive.

Clay fumbled in his pocket and found a quarter. He placed it in the porter's hand. The man glanced down, rolled his eyes and pocketed the coin. "Thenk you, sir," he bowed his head and stalked out.

Clay raced back to the hallway where Evie stood, grinning.

He opened his arms and scooped her up, slamming the door behind him with his foot. As they approached the bed his bad knee gave way, and he tripped, flinging her high in the air. She landed in the center of the bed, eyes, and mouth open wide.

"Oh, honey! I'm sorry." He leaped up, mortified. How could he drop Evie? He placed his good knee on the corner of the bed and approached carefully. "Are you okay?"

But she just giggled and pulled him down by the lapel of his suit.

"Come here, Clay David. How sorry are you?"

"Very, very sorry," he whispered, stroking her hair back from her face.

Her hand touched his cheek, and he covered hers with his own. He kissed her warm mouth and found himself pulled irresistibly into her heartbeat. His own heart pounded until he found himself lightheaded and struggling for air. He rolled onto his back.

"Wait, Ev. I can't breathe..."

"Are you okay?" she jumped up and ran to the bathroom returning with a glass of water. "Here," she helped him sit up and take a sip.

It was lukewarm, but it helped. He inhaled and covered his heart with his hand. He could feel the staccato beat as it skipped and then tried to recover by thumping twice.

"Should we see a doctor?"

"No, I'm fine. I just need to catch my breath."

She sat on the edge of the bed pursing her lips as though she wanted to say something but couldn't figure out how.

"Listen, Clay. We don't need to hurry."

He sat up. His heartbeat seemed to regulate. He drew in a big breath and let it out. "I'm okay. Really."

She turned to him, tears welling, then splashing. "I don't want to lose you, Clay David."

"Not a chance," he whispered gathering her in his arms. Her hair smelled faintly of roses. He closed his eyes and breathed her in. A stray lock tickled his nose. He smiled and rubbed before he could sneeze.

She settled into his side and placed her small hand on his chest. "You keep going in there," she unbuttoned his shirt. "I need him to be with me for a long, long time."

Clay lay back on the bed and pulled her to him.

And for the first time in his life, he felt like a man.

• CHAPTER 22 •

Man-killer

They had not been back from the honeymoon for more than a month when Evelyn started badgering Clay about his father.

"I want you to patch things up."

"There's no patchin'," he insisted. "I want nuthin' to do with him."

"Clay. Christmas is coming. It's a time for family. Won't you try once more? For me?"

He exhaled. "All right Ev. For you. I'll try one more time."

They went the next Sunday. Clay hoped his father would be sober, out of respect for Evie if nothing else. He should have known better.

"I wanna' show you my new horse, Clay. He is my once in a lifetime horse. My reputation maker! He's out here," Milton fairly danced ahead of them he was so excited. "Got him yesterday."

They followed him around the barn to the round pen where Clay saw the scariest looking horse he'd ever seen. Part draft for sure, what else Clay couldn't tell. Huge feet, massive neck. And he was a stallion.

"Got him cheap," his father gloated. "Those saps at the auction house were afraid of him." He picked up his bullwhip and coiled it slowly. "He just hasn't met his match."

As Clay's father approached the pen, the stallion turned and faced him. Not preparing to flee.

"Let me show you how real horse training is done, young lady." He winked at Evelyn, his eyes sliding down her slim body appreciatively.

Evelyn caught Clay's eye. He motioned her to get behind him. She gripped Clay's hand and stepped back.

"No, Dad," Clay said, "that horse is dangerous."

"Nuthin' a good go round won't fix," Milton assured him, slapping his open palm with the bullwhip. "I know how to break a horse, son. None of that touchy feely stuff you do. He needs a good kick in the rear."

Eighteen years of rage flowed through Clay, and he raised his hands. "Let him go. Let him do it. I don't want to watch." He grabbed Ev's hand, and they started towards the truck.

"I hope he kills you!" Clay shouted, turning toward the round pen. The words sounded good coming out of his mouth.

He felt powerful. Tellin' his father what he really thought – for once.

"Let's go, Ev," he said. "We don't need to see this."

She nodded.

He had just closed her door behind her when he heard the horse scream. Clay had never heard a sound like that come from a horse. It raised the hairs on the back of his neck. He raced back around the barn.

Where was his father?

"Oh, God, he's down," Clay breathed.

He flew through the round pen gate, leaving it open behind him. Clay felt the horse race past him, kicking out as it galloped through the gate. His father's body lay crumpled near the snubbing post in the center.

The sight stopped Clay in his tracks.

Blood. So much blood.

It looked like the stallion had kicked him in the face just below his eyes. From the eyes down - he couldn't even look.

"Evelyn!" Clay shouted, "Go get help!"

He heard her speed away in the truck and felt utterly helpless.

He had to do something.

But what?

Clay had never seen anything like it. No way to stop the bleeding. Nothing to be done.

He knelt next to Milton and sought his eyes.

Milton's hand, bloody and trembling, fumbled for Clay's fingers. Clay squeezed his hand and stared at what was left of his father's face.

Milton's nose was gone; his mouth and chin, crushed. His eyes were huge and terrified, but as Clay watched, his eyes became soft. Tears spilled from them, running into the sand.

He stared at Clay, reached up with his hand and touched his cheek.

"I'm sorry, Dad," Clay sobbed.

His father shook his head and then went still, his hand dropping limply by his side, his pupils dilating, his life flowing into the sand.

You killed your father.

Clay received the thought and nodded in agreement. He had killed his father.

God help me.

• CHAPTER 23 •

Back at the Ranch Again

Clay stared into the night sky. The air had cooled, and the stars were bright. He shuddered and rubbed his bare arms. His exposed skin felt hot and tight.

Dang. Hadn't even thought about sunscreen.

He longed to be sleepy but was too agitated.

He reached for the coffee pot, thought better of it and replaced it. "I think I'd better stop if I want to sleep this night."

Gabe leaned forward. "Losing your father that way must have been hard. I'm sorry."

"I still see his face sometimes." Clay shook his head. "Just have to stop thinkin' about it. That Sam Mayfield came through for me. He took care of the funeral, the estate, all the details. He just walked me through it. Got me the best attorney."

"Why did you need an attorney?"

"My father. He got me one last time, from the grave."

"How?"

"There was a will. Left the house and land to Eric first, then Mama. That's it. No mention of me – like I never existed. I had to go to probate court. Not that I wanted to. I was happy to let the land convert to the state of Texas. Never wanted to step foot here," he scanned the barn, "again."

"If you didn't want this, why did you go to court for it?"

"Her," Clay smiled and shrugged one shoulder. "Evie wanted me to have it. She was convinced that God would redeem this place. That it was part of my 'all things,' from Romans Eight."

> *"Clay, it's yours," Evie said. "Rightfully yours. It doesn't matter that your father didn't include you in the will. It's your inheritance. Don't you want it?"*
>
> *He looked at her sweet face, her huge green eyes.*
>
> *"Do you want me to go after it?" he asked.*
>
> *"Yes! I want you to have what is yours!"*
>
> *"I don't care about the land," he whispered, pulling her close. "The only thing I care to have is you."*

"You have me," she grinned. "Let my dad help you to take what is yours. Don't despise what God has provided for you."

"We buried my father, over there, next to Mama," he waved in the general direction of the plot. "I knew I would never live here. Wasn't sure what Evie thought would happen to this place. We didn't really talk about it.

"Within a year, I was approached by some oil prospectors. Mr. Mayfield suggested I hear them out. Was a small group. Two engineers, a driver, and a mud-logger.

"They were just about broke. I felt sorry for 'em, said they could drill a sample hole. I didn't expect them to find anythin', but I had nothing to lose.

"They'd keep most a' the money, but it wouldn't cost me anything if it didn't work.

"They were drivin' to the sample site when the drill truck broke down. They didn't have any money to fix it, and I wasn't spendin' money on a broken truck. They finally drilled where the truck died. Hit one of the largest oil reserves in Central Texas."

Clay stared into his coffee cup. "Here's the funny thing. All the oil found has been on my father's land. The original 5000 acres. We've never found any on what was Mr. Mayfield's land.

And the original spot they prospected didn't have any oil. Not a drop."

Clay shook his head as he looked at Gabe. "That oil changed my life. Gave me money, allowed me to build a real life for Evelyn and me and then Josh."

Clay sipped and looked toward the stars. He could really see Orion.

He tipped his face back toward the fire. "I'd trade everything to see them one more time."

"How long do you think the oil was here before you found it?" Gabe asked.

"I don't know. A long time, I guess."

"Hm," Gabe said like he'd thought about something important, or interesting.

"Hm, what?"

"Your father was a wealthy man, but never experienced it."

"Huh." Clay rubbed his chin. "You're right. Never thought about it that way before."

Clay wondered what Jubilee was doing. Had he found his way to the water?

"You and your father had a lot in common," Gabe said.

That brought Clay back to the conversation, pronto, and he drew himself up. Indignation flared into his chest. "I have *nothing* in common with my father."

Gabe did not seem put off by the anger in Clay's voice. "You are sitting on all the riches of Heaven but don't know it. You are living as though you are in spiritual poverty when you are rich beyond measure."

"What riches of Heaven?" Clay snapped.

"Abundant Life. Jesus said, "I am the Way, the Truth, and the Life."

He's just a kid, Clay reminded himself. He forced himself to breathe. Loosen the shoulders.

"I thought I knew what abundant life was," Clay said. "Those first years everything felt right. I knew what it was to live under God's blessing. Evelyn and I went to church every Sunday, taught Sunday School. I was even a deacon.

"Only thing missin' was children. It didn't bother us at first, but after five years of marriage, and no babies, Evie started gettin' bothered. She'd cry when she saw pregnant ladies at church."

That was your fault too.

"One day she got a phone call from a friend, from her old ballet school in Dallas. Mary was expectin' her first baby, except she wasn't married. She called Ev, all upset, wantin' advice. Evelyn told Mary that we would take her baby if she couldn't keep him. Evie invited that girl to come live with us.

"She didn't even ask me first. She knew I'd say yes. We waited a couple weeks, felt like years, waited for Mary to decide what she would do.

"Finally, Ev couldn't wait any longer, and she called. Mary had already taken care of it. She explained to Evelyn that she didn't want to give up her dancin' career.

"Ev was heartbroken. I had never seen her so broken. She cried for days over that baby."

> *"It's not that I don't have a baby in my arms, that's not why I'm crying, Clay. How could a mother choose death over life for her baby? How? Why would anyone choose death?"*

Clay rubbed his face. Bristly. He swigged the last of his coffee and wiped his mouth with the back of his hand. "We quit talkin' about children. I didn't want to hurt her, so I gave up the idea altogether. I felt lucky to have Evelyn. I didn't need anyone else.

"Sometimes we'd sit on the swing on the front porch. I'd look around at our house, listen to the cows in the pasture, see the horses grazing. I was blessed. And I knew it.

"Whatever I was doin' I guess it was good, 'cause I lived in the land of Milk and Honey. Like it says in the Bible, 'you reap what you sow.'"

"What are you reaping now?"

"Death." He did not hesitate. He knew. "And you know what? I'm not afraid to die...I'm so tired.

"I just don't understand why He would take them. Why them? They didn't do nuthin' wrong. That's the worst. Being left here. Alone."

"What do you think God wants from you?" Gabe's voice was gentle. Not a shred of condemnation.

Clay scratched his head. "I dunno'. Sure wish I knew. So I could do it."

"What if God wants to give you His Life. His Abundant Life. As a gift? What if that's what He's up to?" Gabe sat soft like he had all the time in the world.

"Life?" Clay had to bite down on his tongue, or he'd have said something hateful.

"Only Jesus has the Life. He who has the Son has the Life."

"How do you get the Son?"

"You ask Him."

"I know all this," Clay sneered. "I taught Sunday School for years. But how can God, a God who controls everything, a God who supposedly loves me, how could a good God let all the stuff that's happened, happen. And not just to me. I look around me every day and see more tragedy. It never ends."

"It's true, sir. This world is full of death. It's part of the deal."

"I *hate* that deal." Clay spat.

"Sir," Gabe's eyes glistened. "God hates that deal too. He never wanted His children to enter into Death. But they did.

"God has always been about bringing His kids back into Life. His Life."

"I did choose life," Clay said. "And this is His wonderful plan? No thank you."

"What if," Gabe poked the fire. "What if God's control doesn't look like man's control? What if God's control looks more like provision?"

"Provision?" Clay retorted, glaring toward the burial plot. "This is His provision?"

"What if He has provided Himself? What if God is passionate about relationship?"

"I'm not interested in relationship with a God like that."

Heat rose in Clay's face, and not just from the fire. He moved back into the shadows.

"Your heavenly Father is not like your earthly father, Mr. Westin. He has not left you out of His will."

• CHAPTER 24 •

Thirst

"Listen!" Clay hissed, as he hunkered down and turned his good ear in the direction of the sound.

It was the rhythmic gulping of a thirsty horse drinking. "It's got to be Jube," he whispered, relief bubbling up.

He relaxed his shoulders.

Hadn't even realized he was so tight.

"He'll likely hang around our horses," Gabe said softly. "I put down plenty of hay."

And sure enough, snuffling noises and a low whicker of greeting from Selel.

"Doesn't that make you mad?" Gabe asked, listening to the rustling sounds of horses shifting position.

"What?"

"Doesn't it make you angry that Jubilee is hiding from you?"

Clay crunched up his face. "Angry? Why would that make me mad?"

"Because. He's your horse."

Clay scoffed. "Horses have no notion of ownership. He doesn't know he's mine. He's feeling all alone. That's death to a prey animal."

"Hmmm," Gabe said.

"What do you mean, hmmm."

"People have no notion of ownership either."

"Sure we do. I know he's mine." Clay retorted.

"Ahh, but *whose* are you?"

"What do you mean?"

"You either belong to Death, or you belong to Life. You are either in the first Adam or in the last Adam - Jesus. Which one are you?"

Clay shrugged. "Isn't it clear who I am? I'm a pathetic old sinner – I used to say a sinner saved by grace, but Eli says I've fallen from grace. So I guess I'm just a sinner.

"God has given up on me. And I can't blame Him." Clay wiped his eyes. "I gave up first."

"I see the problem," Gabe whispered.

"Yes – I'm the problem," Clay agreed.

"Your problem, sir, is that you don't know Whose you are – so you don't know who you are. What makes a sinner a sinner?"

Clay stared at him. "Are you really asking me that?"

"Yeah," Gabe replied.

"Sin. That's what makes a sinner a sinner. If it walks like a duck and talks like a duck – it's a duck."

"What verse is that?"

"It's not in the Bible. It's just common sense." Clay huffed.

"So, what makes a horse a horse? Or a grape a grape?"

Clay's frustration rose. "A horse is born a horse."

"Right," Gabe agreed. "Identity is a birth deal. You were born a sinner because you were born in Adam. That was your spiritual DNA. You are a saint because you were born again – into Christ. You are a saint whether you believe it, whether you experience it, or whether you feel it.

"The way God brings His kids back into the Vine is by making them new creations. And guess what sir? When God says something is true, it is true. In fact I think your Abba would ask 'who told you that you were a duck?'" Gabe had a funny half smile.

Clay felt confused. And angry. This young man had some strange and dangerous ideas.

"You know," Gabe continued, "God has given you some pictures of Him in your life. And I don't mean your earthly father. You and Jubilee have much in common, and you have experienced a little taste of your Father's heart for you through Jube."

"What do you mean?"

"Well, you said God has given up on you. Have you given up on Jubilee?"

Clay shook his head. "No! How could I give up on Jube. He's mine. He was Joshie's. He is more valuable to me than anything."

Gabe lifted his eyebrow, "But he's given up on you. He doesn't even want to know you."

"That's not his fault. He's afraid. That's all. Fear has him all muddled inside. He's not thinkin' straight. I can't wait to get him home. Bring him back to who he was."

Rescue. Redemption. Reconciliation. I will always come for you.

"You know, sir. The Christian life isn't difficult. It's impossible."

Clay stared.

Gabe continued. "The Life has only been lived by One. It can still only be lived by One. The question is: does He live in you?"

Clay was suddenly hungry to know more. "Go on."

Gabe stoked the fire again, sending a plume of embers crackling upwards. He grabbed the grape branch from earlier and held it up, inspecting it. The leaves had begun to dry and furl.

"When God made Man in the beginning, He gave them Life. Not just physical life. His Life. Like this branch gets its life from the vine. When Adam and Woman chose to eat from the Tree of Knowledge, they separated themselves from the Father. They chose Death. They thought they could find Life on their own. Apart from God. But there is no Life apart from God."

A warmth flowed deep inside of Clay. A place that had slept for a long time. And he *knew* Gabe's words were true.

"You and Jubilee both belong to love, and have no idea what that means."

Clay could only nod. His heart felt like it would stop. Gabe seemed to be looking straight into him.

Into all his secrets.

"When did Jesus come to save the world?" Gabe asked.

"I don't know," Clay shrugged. "I'm not a history guy. About two thousand years ago I guess."

"In history – you are right. But He is the Lamb, slain from the foundation of the world."

Clay was confused. "How could Jesus be slain from the foundation of the world? Before sin?"

"Because, sir, God is not bound in time. He already knew the choice Adam and Woman would make. He knew they would choose death and He provided the solution. A permanent solution. One that did not depend upon Mankind to fulfill it. He sent the Last Adam, to finish what the first Adam couldn't.

"The deal Jesus made on the cross, was a deal with Death. Not Mankind. Each person needs to decide to reject or receive the deal."

Clay's brow furrowed as his soul shuffled thoughts and beliefs he'd held for decades.

"Here's another question, how many sins did Jesus die for?"

Clay thought. "The ones I confess and repent of," he answered.

"Sir, He died for the sin of the whole world. Everyone's sin. Once, for all."

"Even my dad's sin?"

"Everyone's."

"So how is that fair? I'm here working my butt off, trying to forgive my dad and poof. He's forgiven."

"Forgiveness is a gift, sir. It was given to the world by Jesus. Each person needs to either receive or reject the gift. It is how you can forgive your father for the things he did. By understanding that Jesus paid for it. There is nothing left to be paid."

"I can't forgive him," Clay whispered. "God have mercy on my soul. I can't forgive. I have tried. I know the Bible says that if we won't forgive, we won't be forgiven. I just can't."

"Do you know how far away from you your sin is?" Gabe asked.

"It's all over me," Clay said. "I can feel it, smell it. It walks with me everywhere I go."

"Clay David *Westin*. Your sin is as far from you as the West is from the East. At the bottom of the deep blue sea. Gone.

"Have you ever thought about how far the east is from the west? If you go north long enough, you will eventually be heading south. You can go west forever, and you will never hit east.

"You are free, Sir. Because of Jesus. Jesus is the perfect payment for sin. There can never be any further payment for sin. He chose to die so He would never have to be without you. He will always come for you."

"I wish I could believe you," Clay breathed. "It sounds too good to be true."

Gabe smiled. "That is what He wants you and every child of God to have. Not read about. Not have fleeting glimpses of. He wants to be your Source, your Life."

"Why?" Clay begged, hating the whiny edge to his voice. But he had to know. Desperately. "Why would He do that?"

"Because He loves you. He just loves you. Like you love Jubilee. No matter where he goes, or what he does, you will search for him. Rescue him. Bring him home. Jubilee is the sheep of your pasture. And now you know a tiny piece of the heart of The Shepherd."

Clay allowed that to settle.

"I'm ready," Clay said, inhaling deeply. "Tell me more."

"Tomorrow," Gabe smiled. "It's very late."

Clay looked up at the expanse of stars. The North star seemed to almost vibrate with brightness. He climbed into his bedroll pondering what Gabe had shared. *If You are really here, please show me,* his heart cried.

I AM here. Let me show you.

Clay was in the Garden. He was not certain how he had arrived, but the newness was obvious. Every plant burst with fragrant fruit. The air smelled as pure as baby's breath. A rich carpet of grass beneath his bare feet made each step a delight. Clay stood awhile before his heart fathomed where he was.

Everything, from the stones to himself; everything sang the song of Him. Clay was complete. Loved. Perfectly free. Fearless.

He opened his mouth, and a sound poured from his lips. Joy compelled him, a joy so deep and rich it forced him to sing. He stood, arms outstretched, gazing skyward, the song flowing from him, to Him. All around him Creation answered in a harmonious symphony of voices. All intelligible to Clay. Each bird, every beast, even the trees sang with Clay.

Evelyn, his heart called. He didn't need to open his mouth, he simply thought the thought, and it was expressed.

I'm here, she answered.

He looked but could not see her. He heard her. He walked in the direction of her. She made his heart catch every time he saw her. He walked around a tree and there she was. Laughing, talking, Evelyn, walking with a fawn, her arm draped over its neck. The fawn pressed into her side like a familiar friend. Incandescent light emanated from her; shimmered around her like a ball gown. Clay called to her, and she looked up. Her face glowed as she ran to him. They embraced, then walked hand in hand. Evelyn pulled his hand to her mouth, kissed and released it to dance ahead to pluck a ripe pear from a tree.

Clay called a huge black horse to him. They greeted one another with deep affection. The horse bowed onto his knees inviting Clay to ride. He climbed astride, pulling Evelyn up behind him. They took off together, Evelyn laughing with delight. The horse arched his neck and lifted his tail, expressing his joy in the game. Clay could hear his pleasure.

Clay and Evelyn tumbled off as the black leaped a gooseberry bush. They lay on the ground, unhurt, enjoying the feel of the springy turf on their backs. The horse returned, got down and rolled next to them. The sun shone making their radiance grow even brighter.

Clay rested on his back, hands behind his head. He sighed, utterly content. Then, slowly, drowsily, all three fell asleep in the warm sunshine.

Clay woke hours later. He patted the ground next to him. She was gone.

He rose quickly and began looking for her. He missed her. Wanted to see her.

Ahh, there she was. She was the most beautiful creature he had ever seen. Perfect in form, pure in heart. His joy. They were intimately connected: spiritually, emotionally, physically.

She turned toward him.

Clay recoiled, shocked. She had juice from the fruit of the Tree. The Tree of Knowledge of Good and Evil. The Tree of Death.

The juice ran down her chin, leaving a dark stain. She wiped it with the back of her hand. The stain now spread to her hand and cheek.

"Look! It's good," she cried. "And I did not die. Quickly, eat some. It will make us wise, like God."

He hesitated. He knew he should not but...his love. The love of his life had done this. He could feel the separation occurring even now. Before his eyes she was changing, shrinking, dying. He must eat! Or he would lose her. Unimaginable.

Quickly, before he could think too much, he jammed the fruit into his mouth. It was sweet as it contacted his tongue. He chewed rapidly, then swallowed. Bitterness filled his mouth, ran down his throat. He gathered saliva in his mouth to spit. It didn't matter. The foulness permeated his being. He stood, gasping open mouthed, like a fish on a rock.

Suddenly he was cold. He had never been cold before. It was a dark dead cold that seeped from the very marrow of his bones. No. It was deeper than his bones.

A breeze raised the hairs on his arms. He rubbed his hands over his forearms, staring at them. His flesh had lost its radiance. He looked foreign to himself.

Darkness slid over his eyes, continuing like a shroud, over his brain, clouding his mind. He was disoriented, confused, terrified. He looked for his love. Her radiance too had vanished. He hardly recognized her. She crouched, hunched and miserable. Clay stared around him; nothing looked the same. Nothing sounded the same. The inner connection to his world, his home, was severed.

They blinked at each other with lifeless eyes. Naked. Exposed. Ashamed. Guilty. He had no words for the feelings.

"What did you do?" he whined. He clapped his hand over his mouth. His voice sounded loud, angry. It frightened him.

"Me?" she screamed. "What did you do?"

Clay covered his ears. Her screech made him hurt. All over. He knew he had to hide. Had to hide from her, from himself, most of all from...

"Where are you?"

They heard His familiar voice, only now they jumped with fear instead of joy.

"Hide!" Clay hissed.

They leaped behind a bush together. Clay felt as though his heart would catapult from his chest. Surely He can hear my heart beating.

"Who told you that you were naked?"

Adam and Woman stood before Him, bound together by death, and listened as He explained what they had unleashed. He explained the curse upon the earth. They watched in horror as He killed and skinned the black horse they had ridden earlier. They put on the dripping hide as covering.

All around them they watched the light die. Animals that had crowded around them for love and play now ran in terror. A great chasm opened between God and man. Man and beast. Creatures divided into predator and prey, each focused on its own physical survival. Each the other's enemy.

From the chasm seethed swarms of ticks, mosquitoes and blood-sucking flies.

All creation understood that man had brought Death. That man had destroyed the connection to Life.

The evil one laughed triumphantly as ownership of the world passed to him. He had succeeded in separating God's most precious creation from their source of Life, from their Love.

He had stolen their birthright. And stolen them. They were his slaves, for eternity. And they were not even aware of their bondage. They would serve him and believe they were serving themselves. The brilliance of his scheme was staggering.

Clay stared at Evie. She was all he had left. "You are my life," he proclaimed. "From you I will find my purpose, my significance, my meaning. You will be my source of love."

She stared back, eyes wide. "Me? I thought I was to get those from you?"

"We will fill each other," he assured her.

> *"With what? What is our source?"*
>
> *"We will survive."*
>
> *Clay heard the Father's broken-hearted cry,*
>
> *"We must remove them from The Garden, so they do not eat from the Tree of Life and remain separated forever."*
>
> *So He drove them out. They left the beautiful garden. And set about searching for their lost Life.*

Clay sat up in his bedroll. It was deep night. He took a shaky breath. There was the shell of a house, the horses, the barn. Survive, Clay thought. For what? Not dead, but not living either. He put his head back down on the bedroll, just for a moment...

> *Clay was back in the Garden. There was Jesus hanging on the cross, bloody, exhausted, his face anguished. His blood, mingled with water, poured into the newly created Earth. Clay thought his heart would break. He knew Him and instantly loved Him. Why, Oh, why?*
>
> *And then he knew. My sin. My father's sin. The sin of all Mankind. Paid for, by Jesus.*
>
> *The Rescuer raised His head. He gazed into Clay with such love.*

Clay woke sobbing.

CHAPTER 25

The Round Pen

Gabe rubbed Clay's back and sat with him until he could catch his breath. He brought him a cup of cold water from the well.

"Thank you, son." Clay blew his nose. That dream. He'd never had one so vivid. So real. It felt like he had actually seen Evie again.

Strange. He felt renewed and spent at the same time. Anxious, maybe to get Jubilee and head home.

"We gotta' figger out how to get our hands on him," Clay said.

"What about the round pen?" Gabe suggested. "It's in good shape. You could help him remember. Get him comfortable with you."

"NO!" Clay didn't even have to consider. "I'm not goin' in there."

But the more Clay thought about it the more sense it made. It would make the trip home easier on everyone. Question was, how to get Jubilee in the pen. And quick.

He wanted out of this place.

"Drain the bathtub and put a bucket of water in the round pen," Gabe said, rolling balls of dough and flattening them against the sides of the Dutch oven.

"I know. Let the need draw him." Clay rolled his eyes.

"Exactly." Gabe grinned

Clay huffed, exasperated. Impossible. Thinking about it made him want to puke. It was death. The day his father's blood flowed into the ground. Staining it, staining Clay. Forever.

He busied himself in the old barn instead. Maybe he'd find an old lasso. He stood in front of Shadow's stall. He could make out the "S" he'd dug into the wood of the door. He'd been what – ten? Just a little kid. Clay bent down and touched the rough wood, tracing the crude S shape.

> *Shadow reached over the door and nuzzled his hair with her strong lips. "Cut it out," he giggled, brushing her head away with his hand. He pulled his knife out, determined to carve "Shadow" on her stall door. It would be a work of art. Everyone who saw*

it would know that Shadow was his. That she was loved by him.

"What are you doin' boy?"

Clay jerked upright. "Nothin' sir," he answered, tucking the knife behind his back.

"Don't lie to me."

"I'm, I'm not..."

But even a drunk man could see his handiwork in the wood. Milton grabbed the bull whip from the wall and started toward Shadow.

"No!" Clay screamed, lunging for his father's arm. Milton shook him off easily. He brought his arm back striking the filly again and again. Clay wrapped his thin arms around his father's waist, sobbing hysterically.

"Stop! Stop Dad. Hit me. I'm the liar."

His father's arm dropped. "Quit your cryin'," he commanded, looking at Clay with disgust. "If you ever lie to me again I'll kill her. Do you understand? I'll shoot her dead."

Clay landed on his knees, staring up at his father through tear matted eyelashes. "I promise. I won't lie ever again."

"See that you don't."

Clay wiped his face with his open hand.

Pathetic.

There he was on his sore knees still, cryin'. He'd been crying for 68 years – felt like.

He stared again at the "S" crudely carved in the door. What ever happened to you Shadow? He wondered. I'll never know. I promised I would take care of you.

Liar.

Why would anyone choose death over Life? Ev's words danced through his memory.

I am your Life.

Clay stayed on his knees a moment more. Breathed in. And chose.

"What do I need to do, young man?"

"About what?" Gabe used a stick to pry back the lid, check on the biscuits. He looked up. "Biscuits are almost done." He poured coffee into a cup and offered it to Clay.

"Thanks," Clay sipped carefully. Hot. Very strong. The way he liked.

"Bout the round pen. Usin' it. How do I get myself okay with it?"

Gabe smiled. "Wouldn't be bad to forgive your father. Would likely take all the sting out of that place."

Clay knew that's what the boy would say. He knew it himself. "I'm ready," Clay squeezed his eyelids together as he said it.

Gabe rose. "Shall we?"

As they rounded the back of the barn Clay's knees grew weak and he thought he heard them actually knock together. His stomach went flimsy and he lurched back. "I can't go any farther."

"This is a fine place," Gabe assured him.

"But I can't even see it yet. I just know it's there."

Gabe nodded, "No worries. This is not about the round pen."

Clay's heart pounded so hard, he feared it would leap from his chest. "I can't stay – I'm gonna' puke."

"Sir, you are free. Free to stay, Free to go. This place is not where your bondage lives. The round pen has no power. Your father was not your enemy. The enemy is the enemy and the only power he has is the power you give him."

Clay's legs gave way and he plopped onto the ground. Gabe plopped with him.

"Yer right," he realized, grabbing a ragged breath. "So now what?"

"Your call," Gabe shrugged. "I'm not here to make you do anything. I'm here to walk with you. I am here for you."

"Okay. Let's go." He waited for Gabe to rise, then raised his hand for help.

As they entered the pen, Clay's throat clogged and he could not catch his breath. He leaned into Gabe and his feet stopped. Gabe stopped with him.

"Now what?" Clay choked.

"I would pray, sir. Ask Jesus to heal this memory."

Clay shook his head. He couldn't. "Would you pray for me?"

"Honored, sir." And Clay leaned harder into Gabe's side as the young man prayed. "Lord, Jesus. Thank you for Clay, and his heart for you. Show him the truth about himself, and his father, and this pen."

Clay was enveloped, surrounded by white light, as far as he could see. A tiny dark speck off in the distance caught his attention. The speck grew closer and closer until he could see - a Man. A beautiful Man. With the softest, kindest eyes Clay had ever seen. Eyes more lovely than even Evelyn's.

"Do you want to know the truth about who you are?" The Man asked, His voice as soft as a breeze.

Clay could not answer, but he nodded.

And he saw himself, hanging on a cross. Inside the man. But Clay felt no pain. He just hung there, his heart beating in rhythm with the Man's. Slower and slower until.

Silence.

And then they fell – plummeted straight down.

The earth opened and they plunged into a dark and deep chasm. The air grew cold and still. Like death.

They landed – there was no physical pain. Just darkness. And a cold void, bereft of any light or love or life. Clay could not breathe or feel his heart beat or his blood rush.

Silence, a deafening, overwhelming oblivion entombed him, smothering him, claiming him. He wanted to scream to break the terrible void.

This is what it felt like to be your father. He did not know Life.

Something under Clay leaped upwards.

Like a rocket.

Faster and faster until he felt the skin melting from his flesh. He didn't care.

Exhilaration! He surged upwards, lifting his face, opening his arms, joining the rush.

They erupted from the chasm like a geyser, water splattering all around him, over him. A fountain. A waterfall. Cleansing him.

He landed on the opposite side of the great rift.

Clay planted his feet, amazed by how he felt. How he looked. Clean and radiant. Not just on the outside, but on the inside.

He glanced back, and hanging on the cross, across the chasm, was his old dead self.

"*Now live.*" said the Man. "*I Am your Life, Clay. The strength and quality of our relationship is dependent upon Me and My ability to Love you. Not upon your performance. Do not walk like who you were. Walk like who and Whose you are. New. Free. MINE!*"

"Oh," Clay gasped, and looked down at his legs, straight and strong.

The sand from the round pen came back into view, the bars, the snubbing post.

But his fear had evaporated. Clay shook his head and blinked at Gabe.

Gabe stepped back, arms outstretched. "It's just a round pen, sir."

Clay felt freer than he could ever remember.

And he was finally able to forgive his father.

• CHAPTER 26 •

Bloodlines

Clay pulled the plug in the bathtub, listening as the water trickled out. He filled a bucket halfway and lugged it to the round pen. Biscuits were ready but Clay couldn't eat. Too much on his mind.

He found himself back in the old barn. In front of Shadow's stall. Not sure why.

He bowed his head and closed his eyes. He felt like he should pray, but wasn't sure exactly how the prayer would go. He felt like he wanted to know.

Can You tell me what happened to Shadow?

Will you trust me with her even if you can't see her?

Clay thought about that. *Yes,* his heart replied. *I will trust You, even though I can't see.*

A large wooden crate took up one corner of the stall. Clay cocked his head. Why hadn't he seen it there before? There was no lock, just a clasp.

Opening the lid released the scent of cedar and mothballs. There were dresses. Mama's dresses, tablecloths, curtains. Her old jewelry box on top. When he opened that, a few stray notes of "Amazing Grace" tinkled out. Under the jewelry box were letters. Dozens of them. The paper was yellow and tired, the ink faded. He sat carefully and placed the letters gently on his lap.

A thin unmarked book lay in the very bottom.

Clay opened it and carefully turned the fragile pages. His pulse quickened as he read the first page.

Breeding log for Milton G Westin.

His father's log. The pages were too fragile to flip, he had to carefully read each one before going on to the next.

There! There it was. April 17, 1933. Shadow's birthday.

He ran his finger across the page.

Midnight Jubilee.

Clay held the book in his lap for a moment trying to sort out what that meant.

Midnight. A Jubilee mare?

That meant that Shadow was a Jubilee mare.

Midnight foaled: F for filly. The color: black - going grey. Name: Jubilee's Moonshine. Clay had never heard his father refer to Shadow by that name.

That meant - and he licked his finger and frantically turned the brittle pages to confirm – July 15, 1939; the year his father sold Shadow.

There it was. Jubilee's Moonshine sold to Janice Hart, July 15, 1939. $1500.00. A fortune.

The Harts. A respected family, made famous by breeding the Jubilee line of Quarter Horses near Dallas - for generations.

Clay bought his first Jubilee mare from Janice in 1960 – That mare's dam was Jubilee's Moonshine.

He had bought Shadow's daughter.

His Shadow – one of the most influential mares in history and the great grand-mother of Jube.

He sat back, arms limp. Could it be?

His Shadow.

He still had a little bit of her. And she had not spent years tortured by one of his father's cronies.

She had been loved.

She had been a mother.

He rushed to his feet. He had to tell Gabe.

Clay raced around the side of the barn and there, drinking from the bucket in the round pen, stood Jubilee.

Part Three

• CHAPTER 27 •

Seated In

Gabe handed Clay a biscuit and poured the coffee on the fire. It hissed and popped and brought Clay's mind back to the fire that night.

"I wish He'd a saved Josh," Clay whispered, wiping his eyes. "I would love to talk with him about what's happened. I would have done so many things differently in my life. The fear – that's the biggest thing. I think I would not have been so afraid – to just live."

"Mr. Westin. He did save Josh. And Evie. And you," Gabe replied. "On December 25, 1935, at 10:34 in the morning. Your mother took your hand and led you to Jesus."

Clay couldn't breathe. "How did you know that?" he whispered.

"All the angels in Heaven know that day," Gabe smiled. "We all rejoiced over you."

Clay's lips moved, but no words came.

"May I show you, Sir?" Gabe asked.

Clay nodded.

A silent flash of pure light exploded from Gabe, and they were there.

The first thing Clay noticed was that he felt awake.

Alive.

As though he'd been half asleep his whole life. He had no physical pain. The next thing he noticed was that he wasn't breathing. It felt like when Evelyn took his breath away. It didn't feel strange; indeed, it was wonderful, like he had just taken a drink of mountain air and never needed another.

Clay stared at Gabe who had transformed back into the Archangel Gabriel. He stood over twelve feet tall, his robes and hair the color of lightening.

Clay grabbed his chest.

No heartbeat. *Am I dead*? He hoped. No words came from his mouth, he simply thought the thought, and it was expressed.

Gabriel grinned. No sir! You do not belong to death. This is Life. No heartbeat needed here. Your heartbeat on earth is to remind you of the source of Life. Jesus is your heart.

They stood before a shimmering veil, as intricate and delicate as a spider web. It looked like spun gold with dew dripping from it. It was the most fragile beautiful substance Clay had ever seen. He rubbed it between his fingers. It felt silky, velvety.

On the other side of the veil stood an enormous golden pedestal dripping with jewels and beautiful carvings.

Gabriel walked through the veil and lifted a closed book from the pedestal. As he returned through the veil, the book shrank to the size of an encyclopedia.

The cover radiated white light. From within the whiteness glowed letters inscribed with gold.

Book of Life.

Gabriel opened the book and handed it to Clay. The pages were gold, and he anticipated great weight but it felt buoyant.

And there, in brilliant writing that shone outward like sunlight through a window, was Clay's name, with a date and time. December 25, 1935, 10:34 AM.

And something else.

Beautiful characters, unlike any writing Clay had ever seen. He spread his fingers out and touched his name. Clay David Westin.

"This is His handwriting Clay," said Gabriel. "We celebrated over you on that Christmas."

"All these years I've had this - and didn't know it." The years past seemed like a breath. "What is this next to my name?" He caressed the beautiful writing. "What are these letters?"

"This is the name Father gave you when you became His. It's your true name, one that only He knows. He'll share it with you when it is time. You wouldn't be able to understand it now. Human language does not contain these words. When you hear Him say your name, you will know that it has been your name from before time began."

"Who else is here?" Clay begged, handing the book back.

Gabriel turned the page.

Clay's heart sang. Of course, she was here. "Evelyn Mayfield Westin, 9:14 AM, April 2, 1933. She's here, but... 1933, she was seven years old. How was she Evelyn Mayfield *Westin?*

"Clay," Gabriel clasped his arm gently, "She was yours then. Remember, God is not bound in time. He sees the beginning and the end. When you return, these names will not look the same. You will see only the new names."

"And Josh?"

"Sir, I told you the first day I saw you that I *am* a friend of Joshua's," Gabriel smiled. And there was his name. Joshua Noel Westin. 12:09 PM, May 20, 1980. Clay remembered the day.

Say the words after me, Joshie. "Dear Jesus, come into my heart.

Gabriel turned the page again as he watched Clay's face. Milton George Westin, 2:16 PM, November 3, 1944. The day he died.

Clay stared at him. "My dad? Here?"

Gabriel laughed. "Those last moments, your dad realized he needed saving. Moments are enough time. Your dad received Jesus in the last seconds. You didn't know it, but you and your mother had a profound influence on your father."

"What about Eric? Mama? Pop Mayfield?

"They are all here. They are treasures to store up. Relationships. People. Moth and rust can not destroy them."

Clay peered through the translucence of the veil. The landscape was lush, with plants and animals Clay recognized, and many he did not. In the distance - it had to be a thousand miles - stood a mountain. It had snow just on the top and sat tucked inside a gigantic rainbow.

The rainbow stretched into forever. Clay wasn't sure how he could see into forever, but when he looked at the rainbow, he *knew* that was what he saw. Each primary color had divided into more colors than Clay could count. He simply did not have words to describe the hues.

As Clay concentrated his gaze, the veil became invisible. He could see for thousands of miles. Yet when he focused his eyes, it was as though he was there.

A magnificent white walled city appeared beneath the enormous rainbow. Clay realized that the snow on top of the mountain *was* the city. A single waterfall, hundreds of miles high, cascaded from between two thrones, and fed a wide, smooth river, which ran through the center of the city.

Thousands of people splashed and swam in the river. They stood under the magnificent waterfall. It should have crushed them yet when Clay focused he could see them as clearly as if they were standing right in front of him.

Clay looked back into Gabriel's face. "How many people are in the river?

Gabe glanced over, "three million two thousand and three, that *you* can see. There are many downriver *you* can't see.

"How can you count that many people?" Clay asked astonished.

"I can not only count them, I know them and love them all," Gabriel grinned. "When you return you too will know them and love them. Many will be waiting for you, for your homecoming banquet."

"What do you mean, when I return. Aren't I here?"

"Part of you is here," Gabe nodded. "The part that is connected through Jesus. When you received Jesus, you entered into His life. Jesus is Eternal Life. That's Who He is. You are in Him; He is in you.

"It cannot make sense to you until your mind is completely renewed. That process begins on earth, as much as you will allow. The process will be completed when your time-bound body fails, and you receive your new body. That day is coming, but it is not today."

Voices, millions, billions, reached his ears and he heard them all sing their own personal love song to the One.

Clay caught a familiar face from the corner of his eye.

His father, Milton. But not as Clay remembered him.

Milton's face was passionate, joyful. Life radiated from him. And Mama, her hair long and silky. Her smile. He'd never seen her smile that way.

There were more people, more than Clay could count. The longer he watched, the more details he could see.

Clay looked back at the city. The buildings were bright white, brilliant, incandescent, as though the light glowed from within the stones themselves. He focused and found himself there. It was as though he could see differently, like his eyes worked differently. Everything was clear.

The houses were layered with jewels. Not gaudy; the stones were beautifully arranged, like a lovely mosaic. The streets were paved in - gold.

Even as he thought it he had to smile. "Where the streets are made of gold." Clay's heart understood. The most valuable thing on earth is nothing more than pavement here. Bricks and mortar made from precious elements and jewels. The real treasures are the people.

Inside one of the houses, people were painting. They painted with passion, their brushes flying. Clay gazed at one of the canvases. It was too magnificent for him to describe.

In another room, people wrote. The words flowed onto paper with no effort from the writers. He tried to read one of the manuscripts. The words within the books would have shattered him on earth. The Truth, the Life within. It was too much.

Brightly plumaged birds flew about in groups. Butterflies wafted gently here and there. The flowers were plentiful, and there seemed to be every kind. Tulips, daisies, roses.

Clay could just catch the amazing fragrance. It smelled sweet, not a heavy sweet but a light, delicious aroma. It smelled something like a perfectly ripe peach and pear and melon all together at the same time, each scent unique but in complete harmony with the others.

Lines of heavily fruited trees stretched along the banks of the river. They were perfect and even from the distance Clay could see their fruit, huge, ripe and bountiful.

Clay saw every geography, from tropical rainforests to the tundra. People skied downhill, *without* skis, flying at breakneck speed down mountains thousands of miles high.

Just to the right of the city was a great meadow. In the distance ran herds of large animals, horses perhaps. He would look later, right now Clay saw several children skipping, laughing, singing with total abandon.

It reminded him of Gabe singing 'He leadeth me' in the same rich way.

To the right of the children stood a forest. A forest filled with trees that made the California Redwoods look like saplings. From out of the trees, moving towards the children paced a huge male lion.

Clay saw the lion and part of him knew he should be alarmed, but he wasn't. He felt too safe, too secure. Even a great lion did not frighten him. The beast stopped and from between its front legs stepped a curly-headed toddler.

The lion circled, yawned heavily and laid down. The child curled up and rested his fragile head on the gigantic paw as the lion licked its face tenderly like a mother.

An older child raced toward the resting lion and leaped upon its massive back. The big cat rolled on its back to gaze at the boy with adoration.

Clay's attention came back to the large animals. They *were* horses, with riders on them. One of the riders looked familiar.

It was Josh!

Riding.

Josh grinned, his arms outstretched as they galloped across the plain. The horse, a big black mare had no bridle, no saddle. Clay recognized the mare. Midnight. Pure joy, running together. Samson racing next to them.

Clay felt free, peaceful and wild all at the same time. He reached for the veil, ready to push it aside.

Gabe's hand on his arm stopped him.

"How can I see so far?" Clay asked.

"There are only three dimensions on earth, but Heaven has many more," Gabe explained. "The eyes of your heart are opening. The invisible is becoming visible. And sir, this is just a tiny taste."

Clay reached for the veil again.

"Stop here, sir. You cannot go all the way in," Gabe said.

Why not? Clay's desire was voracious. *I want to go.*

"I know," Gabe acknowledged. "Your time will come. Your journey on earth is not done. You are here for another purpose."

Clay heard music. What was that harmony? A violin, maybe a flute? Whatever it was, its sound was pure, light and lovely. And voices, pure melodic voices joined in.

Clay heard, from every corner, a symphony of voices, and instruments all playing and singing differently, yet as one. Each individual so connected, so in tune with the others, that the different notes melded together perfectly.

A multitude of people danced through the streets of the beautiful city, singing and playing.

And suddenly Evelyn danced from around a corner. She looked like she did when they first married, full of life, a mischievous glow in her eyes. She sang, danced and, leaped at least 20 feet into the air - the most magnificent prima ballerina in the world.

A man danced with her; Clay could only see his back. He stared, *who was that*? He looked strangely familiar.

His mind whirled. The man turned, and Clay recognized … himself.

He was here, dancing with Ev?

He looked at Gabe who shrugged. "I can't explain it to you. It is a mystery too great to comprehend with a time-bound mind. This place is outside of time – you are already seated in the heavenlies. While you are on earth. You'll have to trust that it will make sense when you return.

"In the meantime, know that Evie and Josh are enjoying fellowship with you. Right now."

Then, Evelyn, her face radiant, turned to look back as someone approached.

The crowd parted as the Man walked through. Clay heard their hearts mingling. *Lord! I love You. You are Life to me. Thank You! Praise You forever.*

Clay knew to Whom they sang. He recognized His face.

Tension began to build within him. What will He say? What will He think of me?

Then the beautiful Man with snow-white hair emerged from the throng and looked straight *into* Clay.

His eyes expressed love so deep that Clay dropped to his knees, unable to stand. The Man passed through the veil and stopped in front of Clay. He placed His hand gently on Clay's head.

Then Jesus began to sing over Clay. He sang beautiful words Clay's mind could not comprehend, but his heart and soul drank in. Clay was happy to sit at His feet and allow the words to wash over him.

The words awakened something deep inside of Clay. Not his soul – it was deeper than that. Much deeper.

Clay's sleeping spirit began to stir, and suddenly he understood the words. They penetrated his heart with absolute Truth.

Joy.

Peace.

"*Stand up, Clay,*" Jesus said, holding out His hand.

Clay took His hand and looked up into His eyes. Eyes more beautiful than anything Clay had ever seen.

In an instant, every unfulfilled dream, every hurt, every wound in his soul, healed. The heartbeat that was not in his chest pulsed all around him.

The rhythmic heartbeat of Life-Love, Life-Love, Life-Love, Everlasting. Celestial wings echoed the sound.

All the recognition and love he had felt when he saw Evie and Josh burst a thousand fold. It was a physical sensation, as though his heart had exploded.

Love, pure and overwhelming flowed through him. He was in the presence of Love so strong it made death seem small.

"My Lord," Clay whispered, strengthened by His touch. He stood to be engulfed in His gentle arms.

I have waited for this day, Jesus said.

Clay simply stood, surrounded by His arms, wanting never to leave. Never had he dared to imagine such rest or peace.

I want you to go back.

Clay nodded. Anything Lord. What do you need from me?

Clay, I need nothing from you. I want you to experience my Life, here and on earth.

Do you mean I must leave You? I'll do it if it will help You.

No Clay, you and I will never part. I AM in you, and you are in Me. We are one, inseparable for eternity. I want you to return, to your earthly home. To teach, to share, to love. We will do this together.

I AM your treasure, Clay. I AM your inheritance and your Life forever. Share this Truth with my people. Spread my love to those who do not yet know me. Especially Eli. Eli knows about Me. He reads my Book, he thinks about Me. But he has never invited Me. He does not yet believe.

How will I know what to do?

I AM with you. I will share with you, like a dance, in each heartbeat, each moment. Not before.

Yes, Lord. I am yours.

And I AM yours, Clay David Westin.

And He called Clay by his new name which meant (as close as Clay could translate in earthly language) Most Beloved One.

• CHAPTER 28 •

Shadow

Clay's body jerked awake.

He found himself in the early morning light, near the campfire. He lay still, afraid to move, afraid he would lose the feeling, the peace.

"I was dreamin' I knew it." He felt like weeping.

No Clay, not a dream. Truth.

"Jesus?"

I love you, Clay. I AM here with you. In you. And you are in Me. Inseparable.

I want to live for you, Lord.

Clay, you can't live for me. I AM Life. I want you to live from me. I AM your Source of Life, now and always.

Where is Gabe? I mean Gabriel?

Here, with us.

And Selel – where is she?

Clay looked around. *No Selel.*

"Selel." Clay sucked in his breath with joy.

He understood.

"Selel is Shadow. It's Hebrew for Shadow!"

• CHAPTER 29 •

Remember Me

Go into the round pen.

Clay entered the pen, and Jubilee trotted to the opposite side and then broke into a canter as Clay continued to the center.

Clay invited the horse in, but Jubilee was still too frightened. Too muddled.

Let the need draw him. Pressure reveals the need. The need reveals the source. The source is either sufficient, or it is not.

They had time. All the time in the world.

A horsefly buzzed toward Jubilee, and he broke into a canter.

Flies and lies, Clay. They are similar. They both come from outside. They want to steal your life. You cannot save yourself from the lies. Jubilee cannot save himself from the flies. You need me to save you from lies. Jube needs you to save him. Let the need draw him. That is what need is designed to do. Draw you into Life. He will remember you.

Clay waited, his body soft, heart open. Come Jubilee. I will save you from your tormenter.

Jubilee was tired. His thin body had no strength reserves. In desperation, he turned his eye to Clay who stepped back and invited the horse in.

Suddenly, Clay saw the change. The moment when, through the fog of fear and exhaustion, Jubilee remembered. Clay. His trusted leader. Friend. Fly killer. And the colt whirled in and presented his hindquarters and the fly.

The insect had buried its needle-like nose into the horse and vibrated as it sucked Jube's blood.

Clay smacked it. Hard.

The wrath of God, Clay. You just experienced the wrath. Your wrath is directed at the fly. Not Jubilee. Jubilee can participate in the extermination of the fly. It hurts, but he remembers your heart for him. So he trusts you even when it hurts. He believes that you are for him.

Jubilee sighed and pivoted around to rest his chin on Clay's shoulder – as though nothing had ever happened. Clay threw his arms around the colt's neck.

It's time Clay – time to go home.

Clay walked to the gate, clambered up onto the fence and balanced himself facing Jubilee. Jube followed closely then sidled over to place his body where Clay could climb aboard. Clay grinned, throwing his leg over Jubilee.

Focus on where you want to go. His body will follow yours. You will be as one. Keep your focus on me Clay, and I will direct your steps.

And they were off. Just at a walk. Jube wasn't strong enough to ask for more.

As the ranch house came into view, it began to rain and Jube, recognizing home, broke into a canter.

Clay raised his arms to receive the rain as unspeakable joy filled him. A rainbow burst from the clouds. Clay began singing in a voice rich and melodic. "He leadeth me..."

You are Mine. And I AM yours...

• CHAPTER 30 •

Goin' Home

Spring 2018

Clay woke early, earlier than usual, to watch the remainder of the sunrise. It reminded him of Heaven.

Good morning, Clay.

Morning, Jesus.

Heaven.

No nighttime in Heaven.

No darkness.

Just an ever deeper awareness of the all-consuming, overwhelming, never-ending presence of Father, Jesus, family. Clay couldn't wait to see Ev, Josh, Shadow - everyone.

A string of twelve riders headed out for the day. Their horses looked eager, and Clay heard laughter and conversation in snippets on the breeze.

He smiled, his heart light.

They had just celebrated his 92nd Easter.

They being his dear friend Eli, and Billy, and the 2000 men the Joshua House Prison Ministries had helped. Every one like a son to him. Every single one, dear to his heart.

Jubilee, almost 30, was retired and enjoying life as a World Champion daddy horse. He'd already sired hundreds of Jubilee foals. It made Clay's soul sing to think about Shadow's great-grand-babies.

Clay shook his head and thought of Evie. Couldn't wait to see her again. Still could not figure how he could be laying on this bed with pneumonia while dancing in Heaven, but he knew enough about the invisible to know he didn't need to understand it for it to be true.

He thought back 24 years ago when he had the first Joshua House built. He'd wanted to restore his father's house, but the architect assured him there wasn't enough there to restore. So they'd knocked it down to the foundation stones. And built it new. Looked like the same house. But brand new.

Made him chuckle.

"Good morning, Mr. Westin," Cara greeted, pulling her stethoscope from her neck." She listened to his heart. "Your heart sounds amazing, sir. Strong as a horse. Your lungs are still pretty squeaky though. I want to have the doctor check on you. I'll call him and see if he can swing by later. Can I get you anything?"

"No, Cara. Just sit with me."

She checked his I.V. and pulled a chair closer to his bed.

"I hope you don't mind, sir. I brought my mother to see you."

"Why would I mind? I'd enjoy meeting your mom."

Kristine peeked around the corner of the door. "Hello, Mr. Westin. I don't know if you remember me. It's been a long time."

Her face looked older, but Clay knew her heart instantly. "Kristine! You were with me the day Josh was born." Clay's elation propelled him from his pillow, and he reached for a hug. They embraced carefully, avoiding the I.V. and oxygen lines.

"And Cara is your daughter. I should have known."

Kristine nodded, her eyes shimmery. "Yes, she's my baby."

Cara shook her head, "some baby. Almost 50."

"You'll always be my baby," Kristine smiled. She pulled a chair close to the other side of Clay's bed and held his hand. His fingers still bore the scars from his terrible burns.

"It's the strangest thing, Mr. Westin. Cara told me about you hiring her to take care of you, and we started talking. And realized we were both connected to you. I just felt like there must be a reason. She told me about your son yesterday. Your beautiful boy. I have still never seen a more beautiful baby."

She brushed tears away. "I know it's been twenty-five years since he passed, but I feel like it just happened."

"Time is a funny thing," Clay said, smiling.

"How can you smile about that?" Kristine asked.

"Cara, come and sit. I want to tell you both a story. A true story. Something that happened to me about 24 years ago..."

And they laughed and cried with him as he shared his journey with Gabe and Selel to meet Jesus.

Clay described Jubilee's remembering him in the round pen and suddenly realized how exhausted he was.

Kristine glanced at the clock and gasped, "Oh, my! I've got to get going. I'm working this afternoon. I'm gonna' be late!" She kissed Clay's cheek. "Thank you for sharing with me." She patted his face softly. "I don't think I have the words to tell you how much it meant.

Clay covered her hand with his own. "I'm glad," he whispered. "I'll see you later."

Cara wiped her face with a tissue. "And I need to get you some lunch, Mr. Westin. What would you like? Soup? Burger?"

"Just some tea would be perfect," Clay smiled. "I'm pretty tuckered out."

Cara smiled and glided from the room.

Clay sighed. He was tuckered out.

He closed his eyes, just for a moment.

"Sir?" It was a man's voice. A young man.

Clay knew that voice, and his eyes flew open.

"Hello sir," Gabe grinned. "Want to go for a ride? I've got horses waiting out back."

And Clay leaped from his bed.

O DEATH, WHERE IS YOUR VICTORY?
O DEATH, WHERE IS YOUR STING?
1 Corinthians 15:55

About Jubilee

I originally wanted to set the story in Eden, Texas but there is a real Eden, Texas. I re-worked the letters and came up with Nede. As I researched Nede I found that there existed an ancient tribe of people called the Nedes (or the Nedic people) who did not know their origin. In other words, they didn't know who they were. Clay also did not know who (or Whose) he was. I find most of my struggles begin with this same problem. I do not know who I am because I have forgotten Whose I am.

I began writing Jubilee in 2004, right after I finished Book Four of the Sonrise Farm Series. Jesus placed scenes in my heart and mind, and I wrote furiously to keep up. As I began researching some of the concepts in the book, like the year of Jubilee for example, I was blown away by Leviticus 25:8 ~12

'You are also to count off seven sabbaths of years for yourself, seven times seven years, so that you have the time of the seven sabbaths of years, namely, forty-nine years. You shall then sound a ram's horn abroad on the tenth day of the seventh month; on the day of atonement, you shall sound a horn all through your land. You shall thus consecrate the fiftieth year and proclaim a release through the land to all its inhabitants. It shall be a jubilee for you, and each of you shall return to his own property, and each of you shall return to his family. You shall have the fiftieth year as a jubilee; you shall not sow,

nor reap its after growth, nor gather in from its untrimmed vines. For it is a jubilee; it shall be holy to you. You shall eat its crops out of the field. Leviticus 25:8 ~12 (NASB)

I was not thinking about Leviticus 25 as I wrote the scene at the lake, or Milton's grapes, or many other references to the Biblical Jubilee. I am convinced that Jesus gave me the pictures and the confirmation AFTER I wrote the scene.

I had a similar experience with the Heaven scene. I had read Revelation, but it was not what I was thinking about as I wrote about Clay in Heaven. I simply wrote the images in my head. To read Revelation 21 and 22, where John describes details of Heaven, was overwhelming.

I believe good story should bring us to the finished-ness of redemption. Jesus is the Alpha (Beginning) and Omega (End). He has already seen and made perfect provision for me, no matter what occurs.

Good story should provide hope and peace because it draws us to the Source of Hope and Peace. Jesus.

Here is to Life ~ His Abundant Life!

I hope this is just the beginning of a conversation between us. You can find me here: wwww.KatyPistole.com

ABOUT THE AUTHOR

Katy Pistole has belonged to Jesus since she was 12 years old. Katy has shared the Life and Truth of Jesus as a discipleship counselor and speaker since 2003. Today she loves to share His truth through words, written and spoken.

Katy and her ministry, Beautiful Brokenness, reside in Central Virginia.